我是傑克，
完美馬屁精

文◎安德魯·克萊門斯
譯◎陳雅茜　圖◎唐唐

國家圖書館出版品預行編目（CIP）資料

我是傑克,完美馬屁精 / 安德魯.克萊門斯（Andrew
　Clements）文;陳雅茜譯;唐唐圖. --初版. --臺北市:
　遠流, 2014.01
　　面;　公分. --（安德魯.克萊門斯; 14）
　譯自 : Jake Drake, teacher's pet
　ISBN 978-957-32-7338-7（平裝附光碟片）

874.59　　　　　　　　　　　　102025913

安德魯‧克萊門斯14
我是傑克，完美馬屁精

文 / 安德魯‧克萊門斯　譯 / 陳雅茜　圖 / 唐唐

主編 / 林孜懃　編輯協力 / 陳懿文　內頁設計 / 邱銳致
行銷企劃 / 陳佳美　出版一部總編輯暨總監 / 王明雪

發行人 / 王榮文
出版發行 / 遠流出版事業股份有限公司　104005 台北市中山北路一段11號13樓
電話：(02)2571-0297　傳眞：(02)2571-0197　郵撥：0189456-1
著作權顧問 / 蕭雄淋律師
輸出印刷 / 中原造像股份有限公司
□ 2014年1月1日　初版一刷　□ 2022年8月25日　初版七刷

定價 / 新台幣260元 (缺頁或破損的書，請寄回更換)
有著作權‧侵害必究　Printed in Taiwan
ISBN　978-957-32-7338-7
遠流博識網 http://www.ylib.com　E-mail:ylib@ylib.com
遠流YA讀報粉絲團 https://www.facebook.com/yaread

【推薦導讀一】
進入兒童的大人世界

實踐大學應外系講座教授

陳超明

在《傑克與魔豆》的童話故事中，聰明伶俐的傑克（Jack），運用智慧，巧奪巨人的財富；而在現今的校園裡，不同的傑克（Jake），也面臨不一樣的巨人，正要開始現實生活的冒險之旅。

當自己故事的主人翁

每個人小時候，大都擁有聽大人說故事或自己讀故事的喜悅！沉浸在故事的幻想世界裡，不管是小飛俠彼得潘在森林飛舞，還是孫悟空作弄不同妖魔鬼怪，或傑克與巨人間的最後對抗，我們小小的心靈，都暫時脫離父母的嘮叨、學校作業的負擔、隔壁小胖的霸凌，愉快的當自己的主人翁。

3

從另一面看事情，問題就解決了

故事永遠是我們心靈的好夥伴；好的故事，更是我們展現想像力的好場所！將故事結合現實面，這套【我是傑克】系列，帶我們進入「兒童的大人世界」。我們跟隨著主人翁傑克，有如巨人世界的傑克般，進入各種學校與生活冒險。聰明善良的傑克不斷摸索，發掘事情的另一面，找到破解的方法。

大家常常說，小孩是個無憂無慮的天使。真的是如此嗎？這些故事顛覆了我們大人的看法。回想一下，我們小時候在學校裡，是不是也要面對很多成長的挑戰：不同階段的霸凌、太聰明或太愚蠢的煩惱、同學老師的排擠或另眼相看？故事裡，傑克願意面對自己的問題，也認識自己有限的能力。故事中常不經意的批評大人的輕忽與便宜行事，往往成為小孩世界的夢魘。

迷人的說故事能力

作者是個說故事高手，以第一人稱的敘述觀點進入小孩的世界，勾劃出這些學校的夢魘，更製造層層高潮，吸引我們閱讀：傑克如何打敗超級霸凌者？傑克如何對抗「師寶」的封號？傑克如何鍛鍊自己的智力？傑克又如何發現老師的另一面？小孩的「成熟」，對照大人的「無知」，正是這些故事迷人的地方。誠如傑克自己所說，他一直搞不懂，學校這些每天在教導他們的大人不是應該很聰明、很厲害嗎？為什麼他們始終沒辦法解決校園霸凌的問題呢？不管是大人，還是小孩，來閱讀這些小孩或大人間的精采互動，都會覺得非常有趣！

如何閱讀本系列作品

【我是傑克】不僅是教導小孩如何找到解決問題的方法，更是

5

我是傑克，完美馬屁精

學習語言的好故事書。作者簡潔的語言與故事間的精采轉折，都是本書成功的地方。遠流出版，保留其英文原文，是個非常聰明的作法。我們可以閱讀中文，了解故事情節，也可以回頭看英文，品味這些簡潔語言帶來的美感與魅力。例如 "I tried to smile and nod at him, but I know I looked kind of spooked, because I was spooked. And Link could see I was spooked. And he liked it. And that's when I knew I was in big bully-trouble." 短短四句，重複 spooked，一方面交待傑克成為霸凌對象的過程，一方面也點出其內心的驚慌。這種精采句子到處可見，值得細讀。

這是一系列情節緊湊、語言簡潔、啟發性強的少年故事，大人、小孩都可一起閱讀，不但可以幫助你學習語言，也可以協助你好好面對問題、解決問題！

6

【推薦導讀二】

給讀【我是傑克】的你們

兒童文學作家
幸佳慧

親愛的，我猜，你拿到這本書，可能是父母長輩買來或找來給你的，也可能是同學推薦的。不管怎樣，我們因此在這裡、這一頁相遇。你正讀著字，讀著我這個推薦導讀人寫的字……我的工作就是好好的向你介紹這系列的四本書，就像你的一個好朋友發現了好東西時，會急著和你分享一樣。

安德魯・克萊門斯是美國一位擅長寫學校故事的作家，他總能以學生觀點捉摸到學校生活的各種面相，所以他寫的故事在美國很受歡迎。因為小讀者不會覺得作家藉機說道理（我完全可以體會你們聽說教故事的心情，那感覺就像一朵花好端端的被強行帶到沙漠裡一樣，令人煎熬難受），而是懂得你們的處境或心理，隨著你們

我是傑克，完美馬屁精

的眼睛去感受學校會發生的事情。那種感覺，就像作家透過文字的魔法讓你們變成一尾尾小魚，跳入小溪、滑入大海去自在悠游，卻同時能帶領你們看到特別的新景物。

【我是傑克】這系列講的是一個小男生在他小學不同年級所發生的故事，每本書就像一片片不同的海域，讓小魚兒帶著熟悉的安全感與新鮮的好奇心去探索。

《我是傑克，霸凌終結者》是在說鎮上新來的一個小惡霸，而且他偏偏挑中傑克當他欺負的對象。這讓傑克有機會回想自己為何老是成為惡霸磁鐵的原因，並且激起他要當霸凌終結者的鬥志。不知道你有沒有被霸凌或霸凌別人的經驗？我幼稚園時，有好幾次被霸凌的經驗，那種恐怖心情，一直到現在還記著呢。你們呢？有思考過為何會發生霸凌，發生了要怎麼應對嗎？

【推薦導讀二】

《我是傑克，完美馬屁精》這本也是說著我們都熟悉的情境。

我自己就學期間，從幼稚園到博士班都不喜歡那種會巴結老師或討老師歡心的學生，也就是老師眼中的寵物，同學眼中的馬屁精。不過，有時候你偏偏就會被某個老師盯上，他會對你很好，開口閉口都是你，這讓你很困擾，因為你不想被老師馴服、被同學排擠，你想和同學們同一國，卻不知道該怎麼辦？喔，相信我，那可沒那麼簡單，絕對比把期末考考好還要難，但卻有意思極了！

另外，你有沒有過這種經驗？眼前有個大賽，比的正是你的長項，而且獎品非常非常吸引你，為了得獎，你於是進入了一種六親不認、全力以赴，卻又疑神疑鬼的狀態。整個過程很煎熬，考驗著你和家人、同學的關係，也衝擊著自己對自己的信心，但同時一路上也可能出現意外而有趣的路口，等著你轉彎過去！如果有，那你

9

一定要讀《我是傑克，超跩萬事通》這一本。

另一本《我是傑克，天才搞笑王》也描述了我小時候在學校經歷過的事，就是你明明知道在老師面前「乖乖的」便可以沒事，但你還是忍不住「搞怪」。你也知道下一刻因此要惹禍上身，卻意外觀察到老師們有異狀，然後你才慢慢發現，其實他們有另一個不是老師的身份存在。這個新發現讓你重新看待自己和大人的關係，也才知道原來上學這件事有好笑、溫柔與不為人知的一面呢！

總之，我很努力的向你們介紹這四本書有意思且吸引人的地方，希望你接下去有機會翻完它們，並回過頭來評評我分享的話有沒有道理。若覺得沒道理，那也很好，這樣你就可以開始寫你想分享給其他小讀者的推薦導讀了，我可是很樂意拜讀的！

名家好評推薦

乖巧、伶俐，帶著一點膽怯，卻又總是強自鎮定的傑克，和我兒子正好同年，今年十歲，四年級。而且，有點小聰明的性格也有那麼一點類似呢！所以，每當我看到傑克在學校裡遇到麻煩與困擾時，忍不住也會想像，當我兒子遇到同樣情形時，他會怎麼辦？

克萊門斯的作品活潑逗趣，貼近小朋友的想法與經歷，讀來輕鬆愉快，又引人入勝。【我是傑克】系列以中英雙語方式出版，拉長了閱讀年齡層，讓高年級的孩子也可以把它當成一本練習英文的讀本，是相當值得收藏的好書喔！

——親子作家

陳安儀

1 糟糕的四天

我是傑克，全名叫傑克・德瑞克。我現在正好在四年級的中間。關於四年級，我最喜歡的一件事就是，我再也不是幼稚園、一年級、二年級或三年級；還有，我也不必去露露小姐的點心尿布托嬰中心了。

我覺得四年級是我目前為止最好的一個年級，好到我得用力想，才想得出這段時間發生過什麼壞事。就好比現在

嗎？我只想得出曾有過不是那麼好的一天。在那天，我覺得

我的老師湯普森先生不公平。

原因是他那天對待尚恩·安德伍的方式。首先，湯普森

先生指定尚恩帶領大家唸效忠誓詞。接著，湯普森先生派尚

恩把點名表拿去辦公室。數學課時，湯普森先生叫尚恩到黑

板寫答案。上午休息時間過後，湯普森先生讓尚恩為朗讀時

間挑選新的故事書。然後到了午餐時間，湯普森先生又指派

尚恩排在第一個。

我知道這聽起來會讓人覺得我對這些事情太過小題大

作，但尚恩看起來就像是湯普森先生最喜歡的學生，像是尚

恩變成老師的寵物一樣。那並不公平。

但結果是我錯怪尚恩了。那天吃完午餐後，湯普森先生說：「我有好消息和壞消息要告訴大家。好消息是，今天放學前我們要舉辦一個派對，會有蛋糕和冰淇淋。但壞消息是，這將是尚恩的歡送會。明天尚恩就要搬到別州去了，我們以後會很想念他的。」

湯普森先生對尚恩特別好，是因為這是他的最後一天。

所以尚恩並不是老師的寵物。我很高興，因為我喜歡尚恩，而變成老師的寵物，是小孩在學校裡最可怕的遭遇之一。

你知道身為老師的寵物，有什麼好討厭的嗎？每一件事都討厭，就是這樣。

這我當然知道，因為去年五月、就在三年級快結束時，

我是傑克，完美馬屁精

發生了一件事。這件事維持了四天，還不到一星期，但對我來說，那四天感覺卻像四年。因為在那四天裡，我陷入了巨大的危險中。

我有失去朋友的危險、失去名譽的危險，還有失去⋯⋯理智的危險。

因為在那段時間，我變成了老師的寵物，傑克・德瑞克。

三年級那年，我們班上多了五台新電腦。斯納文太太是我三年級的導師，她表現得像電腦是個可怕的東西，特別是新的電腦。她總是得一邊閱讀使用手冊，一邊使用電腦。即使那樣，她還是常把事情弄得一團亂，然後必須打電話給李

18

德太太，也就是圖書管理員，請她過來教她怎麼做。

五月的一個星期一早上，斯納文太太坐在教室後面的一台新電腦前，被我們數學課要用的某個程式弄得糊里糊塗。我的桌子就在電腦附近，而我那時正看著她。

斯納文太太看看螢幕，再看看手冊，然後又看看螢幕。接著她搖搖頭，嘆了一大口氣。我看得出來，她就要打電話給李德太太了。

我一向喜歡電腦，而且知道怎麼用電腦處理一些事，像是開機、啟動程式、玩電動、打字、畫圖，還有建置網頁之類。於是我從自己桌子前站起來，指著電腦螢幕，然後說：

「斯納文太太，如果你在那邊那個小東西上面點兩下滑鼠，程

式就會開始跑。然後你再點一下這個，就可以打開有關數線的部分。」

於是斯納文太太照我說的去做，程式開始跑了起來。因為它就是那樣運作的，大家都知道，除了斯納文太太。

當那個程式開始播放它愚蠢的音樂時，斯納文太太對我露出大大的笑容，並且說：「傑克，你真是**太棒了！**」而且她說得很大聲，**太大聲了**。

她的聲音那麼響亮，所以班上所有孩子都停下手邊的事，轉頭看著我們，剛好看到斯納文太太拍著我的頭，好像我是一隻乖小狗或什麼似的；而且是一隻滿臉通紅又很糗的小狗。

所以我喃喃說著：「喔，沒什麼啦。」這真是個錯誤。

因為她立刻說：「但你錯了，傑克。我在使用這些新電腦時，真的覺得**非常**混亂。想想看，有這麼**棒**的一位專家一直待在我的班上，而我竟然不知道！從現在開始，你就是我的**專任電腦小幫手！**」

我趁她來不及再拍我的頭之前趕快坐下，但最糟的部分還沒發生。因為斯納文太太走到教室前面說：「各位同學，今天下午的數學時間，有任何人在操作電腦時遇到問題，可以問問傑克怎麼做。他是我的專任電腦小幫手！」

這時我的臉已經紅得不得了，連耳朵都開始發燙。我一直盯著桌子，即使如此，我還是知道教室裡的每個人都在看

著我。我等著有人開始嘲笑我，尤其是那些比我更懂電腦的孩子，像是班恩，或是雪莉‧歐卡特。雪莉是我們全校最屬害的電腦專家。

就在這時候，第一節課的鐘聲響起，該去上美術課了。

鐘聲救了我。

那天早上，柯特小姐的教室非常亂，大概因為那樣，所以我總是很喜歡美術教室。這是全校唯一不用擔心整潔的地方，也不必擔心東西濺出來，或擔心要趕快完成功課。

上美術課的第一件事是套上大襯衫，因為理論上它們可以把顏料、膠水和廢棄物擋在我們的衣服外面。我穿上我爸的一件藍色舊襯衫，其他孩子也套上他們的巨大襯衫，所以

我們看起來都變成了短腿一族。這是上美術課的另一項樂趣。

那個星期一，我在窗邊的畫架旁工作。理論上是要畫母親節的圖畫。

大約畫了一半，我覺得自己需要一枝比較小的水彩筆，所以去大水槽那邊找。那裡大概有十五或二十枝水彩筆，全插在一個桶子裡，桶子裡裝滿了棕色加綠色加黃色的水。我抓起一把水彩筆想找出合適的尺寸。然後我感覺身後有人接近，於是加快動作，把所有水彩筆拿到水龍頭下面沖洗，挑出我想要的一枝，接著把其他筆放在水槽上方的架子上。

我看向身後，發現柯特小姐站在那裡。她一臉傻傻的將頭歪向一邊，對著我微笑。

「傑克！這是整個星期以來，有人在這間教室裡所做過**最**貼心的一件事！」那完全沒有道理，因為當時不過是星期一早上，整個星期才剛開始。但我猜柯特小姐並不在意。

我露出無力的微笑，然後說：「我⋯⋯我需要一枝比較小的筆，這樣才能完成⋯⋯」

柯特小姐說：「你沒有趕著完成自己的圖畫，卻停下來幫忙清洗水彩筆！那真是**太貼心**了！」這時候，全班都在盯著我們看，我真希望柯特小姐不要再用那種語氣說「貼心」兩個字。

但是柯特小姐還沒說完。她轉身面對班上所有孩子，並說：「如果你們全都像傑克這麼**貼心**，稍微幫忙清理一下，

這間教室也許就不會總是這麼亂了。**太謝謝你了，傑克！**

柯特小姐一邊這麼說，一邊拍著我的頭。

我抓著小水彩筆，快速回到我的畫架旁邊。我再次開始

畫畫，試著不讓自己感到那麼難為情。

然後我聽到班恩在對馬克說悄悄話。班恩·古朗森除了

對電腦很在行，他大概也是我們三年級班上最惡劣的孩子。

他把悄悄話說得特別大聲，好確定我聽得見。「嘿，馬克，你

不覺得傑克快要變成完美的人了嗎？他好**貼心**喔！」我假裝

沒聽見，但我知道自己的臉變得愈來愈紅。

上完美術課，我們回到自己的教室上閱讀課和社會課。

沒發生什麼事。

接著，就在午餐之前，我們上了體育課。柯林斯先生打算來個「好漢日」。當柯林斯先生想要執行好漢日時，你可以分辨得出來，因為在好漢日，他會用「部隊」來稱呼所有的男生和女生。

鐘響之後，柯林斯先生吹響哨子，大叫：「好，部隊們仔細聽著。在球場中央這裡排成一直線。快點，部隊成員，看起來有活力一點！今天我們要玩⋯⋯躲避球！」

班上有一半的人發出呻吟，另一半發出歡呼。呻吟的是那些常常被大紅球轟到的孩子；歡呼的則是那些很會丟球、接球的孩子。我是呻吟的孩子之一。對我來說，躲避球代表試著活下去。

柯林斯先生拍拍他的手。「好了，部隊們！姓氏的第一個

字母屬於 A 到 L 的人，到球場那邊去。屬於 M 到 Z 的人，

到我後面這邊來。大家快點！快！快！快！」

柯林斯先生沿著體育館中央的黑線把球滾出去，比賽開

始。葛倫‧珀迪跑出來，為我的敵隊抓起球❶。

關於躲避球，有件事……很古怪。我不知道它為什麼能

引出某些孩子最壞的一面，但的確是這樣。以葛倫‧珀迪來

說，在真實的生活裡，他是個相當好的孩子。他很友善，也

是數學課或閱讀課的好搭檔，而且在籃球比賽時，有他當隊

❶ 傑克‧德瑞克的英文名是Jake Drake，所以姓氏第一個字母為D。葛倫‧珀
迪英文名是Glen Purdy，姓氏第一個字母為P，所以和傑克分在不同隊伍。

27

友很好，因為他長得很高。

但只要躲避球賽一開始，這個好人就會突然變成一頭野獸。而且他的手臂很長，所以當他擲出大紅球時，那顆球就好像是從大炮裡射出來的一樣。

所以葛倫一拿到球，我們全隊立刻往後退到牆邊。我們知道葛倫一定會轟倒某個人，而且他真的做到了。

就是我。正中肩膀。

大概只花了四分鐘，我隊上的其他人就全部被打出場，然後柯林斯先生拍拍他的手，說：「來，部隊成員們，再來一次。這次用兩顆球來比賽。」

然後他把兩顆球沿著黑色的中線滾出去。

這表示，現在有某個孩子可能同時被**兩顆**大紅球轟倒。

而且真的發生了，就發生在我身上，而且再次發生在第一次擲球的時候。一顆球打中我的腳踝，另一顆打中我的肚子。

那天接下來的四場躲避球賽，對我來說就像這樣：轟！

轟！轟！轟！總共有六場躲避球賽，每一場我都是第一個被打倒的孩子。

但是當第三次被球轟倒、膝蓋擦破皮時，我有要求去找保健室的阿姨嗎？沒有。當第五次被球轟倒、正中腦袋、頓時看到滿天小小彩虹時，我有要求躺在墊子上休息嗎？沒有。為什麼？也許因為我很笨，但很可能是因為，就算我不是重要的人物，即使有時受了傷，我也不希望有人認為我是

半途而廢的人。

無論如何，當體育課終於結束，大家在門邊排隊時，我真的好高興自己排在最前面，可以第一個解散去吃午餐。

柯林斯先生走向門口，哨子用力一吹，要每個人安靜下來。然後他說：「聽著，部隊們。今天大家表現得很好、很讚。不過本日最佳球員獎，也許連本月最佳球員獎，都要頒發給某個特別的同學。大家有沒有發現，有個人在今天的每一場比賽都是第一個被打到，但是那個人有抱怨嗎？沒有。他有發牢騷或呻吟嗎？沒有。為什麼？因為他是真正的部隊人，這就是原因。傑克‧德瑞克值得我頒發體育榮譽獎章給他，大家可以從他身上學習到如何成為一名具有運動精神的

人。好了，部隊們，解散！」

而且當然了，柯林斯先生一邊說到我的時候，一邊在做

什麼呢？他在拍我的頭。當他說話時，我看著其他孩子。看

得出來，他們並不認為我應該因為躲避球比賽表現得很差，

而獲得所有關注。

站在體育館的門邊，柯林斯先生拍著我的頭，讓我空盪

盪的胃裡有種下沉的感覺。

因為星期一才過了一半，而我已經快要變成戴普雷小學

史上最不受歡迎的孩子了。

2 垃圾男孩

體育課之後，我回到教室拿我的午餐袋，然後急忙趕去餐廳。我想和威利坐在一起，他是我最好的朋友。威利的真名叫做菲爾，但姓氏是威利斯，所以每個人都叫他威利。我們三年級那年，他被分到佛魯太太的班上，所以我只能在午餐和下課時間見到他。

「嗨，威利。」我把午餐放在桌上，然後去排隊拿牛奶。

我站在那裡隨意看著一張桌子，看到了我們班的兩個女生，瑪莎和珍。瑪莎正看著我和珍說悄悄話，然後珍看著我，她們又看著彼此，接著兩人開始哈哈笑。我不喜歡她們哈哈笑的樣子，卻什麼都不能做，所以我拿了威利和自己的牛奶準備回去坐下。

要走回座位，我必須先經過班恩·古朗森。他和卡爾·伯頓站在午餐隊伍的最後面。當我走過班恩身邊，他對卡爾咧嘴一笑，並說：「嘿，看，是傑克。他是真正的**部隊人**耶，你知道的，而且還很**貼心**。」雖然卡爾是我的朋友，他還是哈哈大笑了。我不怪他，我猜這**真的**很好笑。在那個當下，只有我不覺得有趣。我咬咬牙，走回威利坐的那張桌子。

34

威利朝著班恩點點頭，說：「那是什麼狀況？」

「那個嗎？」我說：「沒什麼啦。今天上體育課時，一連六場躲避球賽，我都是第一個被打到的人。」然後柯林斯先生對這件事情大驚小怪的。所以班恩在嘲笑我。」

威利做了一個鬼臉。「你怎麼受得了和班恩同班呢？他真是個混蛋。」

「對呀，」我同意，「他確實是。」

之後我們開始討論我們都想要的電腦遊戲，這樣我們在家才能連線和對方一起玩。所以午餐很棒，因為和威利聊天一向很有趣，也因為我不必再擔心自己的頭被大紅球轟到。

吃完餅乾後，我說：「來吧。」對威利和我來說，這句話

我是傑克，完美馬屁精

表示該玩「剪刀、石頭、布」了。因為每天吃完午餐，我們

都會猜三次剪刀、石頭、布，看誰必須把垃圾拿去垃圾桶。

我贏了第一次，但威利贏了接下來的兩次。他笑著說：

「我得拿一本書去圖書館還，所以也許放學之後再見。」

我開始清理桌面。威利不是那種吃相很好的人，他的橘

子皮剝得到處都是，有些薯片在他打開包裝袋時掉了出來。

另外，他還灑出一些巧克力牛奶。

所以我站起身，拿一些紙巾，傾身把對面桌上的牛奶擦

乾淨。這時我突然聽到有個聲音從我身後傳來，這是會讓戴

普雷小學的每個小孩都嚇一大跳的聲音。

「你！那邊那個！」

36

我的心臟幾乎快從嘴裡跳出來。因為在我們學校只有一

個人有這樣的聲音，那就是卡普太太，我們的校長。

「住手，把東西放下，立正站好！」卡普太太幾乎是用吼

的，所以整個餐廳變得安靜無聲。她的聲音是會把幼稚園小

孩嚇哭的那種，而且聲音大到讓我覺得她如果真的大吼起

來，一定可以把窗戶震破。

卡普太太走過來，站在我身邊。她環視全場，確定餐廳

裡的每個人都有注意聽，然後她用響亮的聲音說：「每一天，

我們的餐廳助手在午餐之後都得花額外的時間清理這裡。仔

細看看這張桌子。」她指著我面前那團髒亂，有兩個揉皺的午

餐袋、一個壓扁的巧克力牛奶盒、三根彎曲的吸管、一疊溼

答答的紙巾，還有一堆橘子皮和薯片。不是很美觀的畫面。

我憋著一口氣，嚇得動彈不得。接著卡普太太說：「傑克．德瑞克不只是開始清理自己的東西，還幫忙清理某個**壞**公民留下的髒亂。」

我抬起頭，看到威利正站在門邊——壞公民威利。他對我露出一臉驚嚇的表情，好像以為我會指著他說：「他在那裡！」但我絕不會那麼做。

卡普太太手裡拿著某種東西，是巡邏帶，指揮大家過馬路的警衛穿的那種。她朝著我彎下腰，我什麼都來不及做，她就把那條帶子套過我的頭，環在我的腰上扣了起來。那東西對我來說太大了，只能整個垂掛在那裡。接著她笑著說：

「看到這條巡邏帶了嗎？」這真是個蠢問題，因為那東西是亮橘色的，根本不可能**看不見**。「這個星期我們要特別多花些力氣保持餐廳的整潔。本週接下來的每一天，傑克‧德瑞克將在午餐時間戴上這條帶子，幫忙提醒我們所有人，不要把**任何垃圾留在桌上**。傑克是優秀的餐廳公民，我希望大家給他熱烈的掌聲。傑克，你為大家樹立了良好的模範！」

接著，卡普太太開始鼓掌，並且環視餐廳，所以其他人也都必須鼓掌。我看到威利站在門口，像瘋了一樣的拍著手，並且咧嘴對我笑。

當每個人都在鼓掌時，卡普太太在做什麼呢？她不再鼓掌，而是伸出手來，在三、四、五年級所有孩子的注目下，

拍著我的頭。

掌聲停止了，卡普太太再次對我笑一笑，然後離開。我把午餐的桌子清理乾淨，努力忽視那種大家都在看我的感覺。但是當你戴著一條又大又鬆的橘色巡邏帶時，真的很不容易做到。我迅速離開餐廳。

威利在走廊上等我。他指著那條橘色腰帶，裝出一副好像它很神奇的樣子。他把眼睛張得大大的說：「天啊！我可以摸一下嗎？」

我可沒笑，直接走過他身邊，因為我得快點回去斯納文太太的教室，才能把那個蠢東西拿下來，塞到桌子裡面。

威利追了上來說：「別生氣啦，傑克。我只是在開玩笑。」

「嗯，這並不好笑。」我說。我不喜歡現在發生的事。

午休時間結束後，班上所有的孩子都回到了教室。我們坐下來，拿出數學習作。斯納文太太等所有孩子都安靜坐好，然後說：「在我們開始上數學之前，我需要有人幫我把這張便條紙拿到辦公室。」

大概有六個孩子立刻舉手，因為有些孩子就是喜歡做這種事。斯納文太太的視線直接穿過那些揮舞的手。她看著我，並笑著說：「我想請傑克幫忙拿過去。」她伸手把便條遞給我，我只好從座位上站起來，走到教室前面，從她那裡接過便條紙。然後斯納文太太說：「不過一定要馬上回來，傑克，因為我們就要開始做數線的題目了。你必須擔任我的**專**

任電腦小幫手，好嗎？」我感覺到全班每個孩子都在看我。

他們什麼都沒說，甚至連悄悄話也沒有。但就在那時候，我卻聽到了他們的想法。他們心裡想著：老師的寵物。

斯納文太太一點都沒有幫到忙。在那天最後的兩個小時裡，她一直要我提醒她怎麼在電腦上做各種不同的事，或者要我去協助這個孩子，然後又協助那個孩子。最糟的是，沒有人真的需要協助，他們也不想被協助，特別是來自老師寵物的幫忙。輪到我使用電腦時，斯納文太太跑過來看我，然後說：「能看到一位真正的**專家**操作這個數學程式，真是太棒了！」我覺得那天永遠不會結束。

但它確實結束了。當我終於跑出學校等公車時，心情非

常糟。我站在隊伍中，一位五年級的男生走過來說：「嘿，垃圾男孩！我想卡普太太愛上你了！」

接著他的朋友全都哈哈大笑，然後另一個孩子說：「對，垃圾男孩！也許明天你可以來清理**我的**餐桌。要清乾淨喔，因為你不想惹校長不高興吧！」

三號公車來了，我上了車，坐在其中一個座位的外側，免得有人過來跟我坐在一起。我不想和任何人講話，我只是坐在那裡，盯著骯髒的黑色地板看。我身邊的孩子們都在聊天、開玩笑、大吼大叫、哈哈大笑。我沒有。

我感覺很糟。這不公平。我並不想當老師的寵物，也不曾試著引起任何人的注意。那不是我的錯。我感覺自己被困

住了。

我抬頭一看，下一站就是我要下車的地方。公車停下來時，我跳起來走到公車前面，想要第一個下車。我想快點讓今天結束。

車子裡真的很吵，駕駛公車的女士從座位上轉身大吼：

「安靜！」

等到所有人都不再吼叫、講話，司機才看著大家說：「你們這些小孩乖一點！在這麼吵鬧的環境裡開車並不安全。你們應該在座位上坐好，如果要講話，就講小聲一點，懂了嗎？今天在這輛公車裡，就只有一個孩子稱得上是好乘客，就是這裡的這位。」

然後那位公車司機當著所有孩子的面伸出手，拍一拍我的頭。

3 特殊待遇

那天下午回家之後，我直接上樓進房間，甚至連點心都沒吃。

所以媽媽跟在我後面，進到我房間，然後說：「傑克，你還好嗎？」

我不知道該怎麼解釋。因為如果我對她說：「所有的老師都覺得我很棒，就連校長也是。」那麼我媽一定會說：

「嗯，你**的確**很棒呀，傑克！」或其他類似的話。因為做媽媽的就是這樣。

所以我說：「我沒事，媽。只是今天在學校有點累。」那是實話。當學校裡的每個孩子都以為你想變成老師的寵物，的確會讓人覺得很累。而且被躲避球轟到六、七次，更不會有什麼有幫助。

不過晚餐之後，我們看了有關海岸防衛隊的電視節目，內容很精采，所以我不再想起學校的事，心裡覺得好過一點。

爸爸唸完一章床邊故事之後，幫我把被子塞好，親了我一下說晚安，然後關燈，這時我忍不住又想起學校的事。我告訴自己，那大概只是一個可怕的星期一罷了，靠著這種方

法，我才終於睡著。我告訴自己，明天一切都會恢復正常；明天，我會變回一個普通的小孩。我那麼告訴自己，而且希望能夠成真。我想要它成真，我需要它成真。帶著這種深信不疑的心情，我睡著了。

星期二搭公車去上學時，一切都很好。我只是一個小孩，不太吵也不太安靜。公車司機甚至沒注意到我在那裡，而且沒有任何人提起星期一發生的事。我告訴自己：看到了嗎？沒什麼好擔心的。

但這句話說得太快。我一走進斯納文太太的教室，她就說：「喔，好極了！你來了，傑克。沒有**我的專任**電腦小幫

手，我真不知道要怎麼活過另一天！」然後她指著她的電腦螢幕說：「我已經把那個數學程式打開，不過它恐怕又被我弄亂了。你能過來這裡看看我有沒有做對嗎？」她沒做對，所以我必須幫忙把它調整好。調好之後，斯納文太太說：「傑克，你又救了我一次！」

那時，其他孩子幾乎都已經進了教室。我感覺得到他們在看我，而且看得出來他們在想的事：是老師的寵物呢，已經在努力工作了！

狀況看起來真的就是那樣。因為斯納文太太要誰把點名表拿去辦公室呢？我。到了閱讀時間，斯納文太太最先叫誰起來大聲朗誦呢？我。然後當大家排隊要去禮堂開集會時，

特殊待遇

斯納文太太又選誰排在隊伍的最前面呢？我。

這次的集會大家期待了好久，因為有一位女士會來，她自稱是「說故事的拇指姑娘」。她以前也來學校表演過，很精采。她會說故事，但不是只把故事讀一讀而已，而是一個人演出故事的所有情節。她有一大堆不同的戲服、帽子、鬍子和假髮，還有好幾個大籃子，裡面裝滿劍、繩子和燈籠之類的東西。如果故事裡提到城堡，她就會從籃子裡拿出一片城牆，讓你相信那裡真的有一座城堡。

我很高興拇指姑娘那個星期二來表演。那時才早上十點半，但我已經需要休息了。我想要和三、四、五年級所有孩子一起坐在大廳裡，然後等禮堂的燈光一暗，我就可以消失

51

在人群之中，享受表演。

拇指姑娘上台了，我們全都開始拍手。她戴著長長的紅色假髮，低頭一鞠躬，接著說：「早安！今天一開始，我要先講一個很久很久以前的故事。為了講這個故事，我需要一個幫手，這個人必須忠實、純真、誠實、品性良好，是一個穿著發亮盔甲的真正騎士。」然後她伸出一隻手遮在前額上，好擋住眼前的強光，另一隻手則指向觀眾。

她指著坐在我正前方的一個四年級學生。「那位同學！」

她說：「我覺得你看起來很像王子！快上台來協助我講故事吧！」那個孩子開始搖頭說不，我對他感到很同情。

突然，斯納文太太來到我身邊。她說：「傑克！你是幫

忙她的**最佳人選**！」她說得好大聲，而且還抓起我的手，把我從座位上拉起來。拇指姑娘一看到我站起來，立刻拍手說：「太棒了！我們的王子出現了！」

十五秒後，我已經在舞台上走著，並且瘋狂的眨著眼，努力避免被滿地的道具絆倒。

當你面臨生命中最糟糕的十分鐘，任誰也沒辦法提前做好準備。前一分鐘，我還坐在黑暗中享受表演；後一分鐘，我**成了**表演的一部分。而這位戴著大頂假髮的女士在我頭上扣了一頂騎士頭盔，並且拿塑膠盔甲包住我的胸口，然後遞給我一把長劍。如果眼前沒有四百位孩子在嘲笑我，那把劍揮起來應該會滿有趣的。

53

接著，拇指姑娘又把一個東西套在我身上，應該是一匹馬。前面有馬頭，後面是馬屁股和尾巴，中間則是留給我的空間。整個道具以兩條帶子掛在我的肩上。為了讓馬動起來，我得「答啦！答啦！答啦！」的跑來跑去。

她一邊把那匹馬掛在我身上，一邊說：「好了，你只需要這麼做：先在簾幕後面等著，只要我一說：『有人會來救我！』你就騎著馬跑過舞台，從我身邊經過。而且你要一邊揮劍，一邊大喊：『我來救你了，公主！』接著，到另一邊的簾幕後面等著。當我再次說出那句台詞時，你再跑出來，重複相同的動作。好嗎？」

我點點頭說：「好。」因為我已經被綁在戲服裡了，而那

位女士也已經準備好要開始。我還能做什麼呢？

我躲在簾幕後面，拇指姑娘開始說故事。隨著故事的進展，她大概說了二十次：「有人會來救我！」接著這位愚蠢的騎士就得騎馬跑過舞台，大喊著：「我來救你了，公主！」那是個大笑話，那就是我，我就是那個愚蠢的大笑話。

最後，故事結束了。拇指姑娘要我和我的馬來到舞台中央。我得握住她的手，然後鞠躬。接著，我騎馬跑到簾幕後面，大概花了三秒鐘就把那套戲服脫下來。

我想我那天臉紅的次數一定創了新紀錄。雖然舞台上有表演正在進行，但每次我環顧四周，總覺得觀眾席裡有一半的孩子在看我。我試著不要去注意，還真的有效，因為過了

一會兒之後，我真的忘了舞台上那段可怕的時光。我和其他人一樣，欣賞接下來的故事。

最後一個故事說完後，每個人都瘋狂鼓掌。那真是很棒的一次集會。所有老師都站了起來，卡普太太走上舞台，舉起手，掌聲停了下來。

卡普太太說：「拇指姑娘今天的表演真是太令人享受了，我知道這句話是我們每一個人的心聲。讓我們再一次給她熱烈的掌聲。」

所以我們全都開始再次鼓掌、歡呼。接著，卡普太太又舉起手，喧鬧聲立刻停止，就像電視機被關掉一樣。

卡普太太說：「趁我還沒忘記之前，傑克，你能回到舞

「台上嗎？」

整個禮堂變得安靜無比，只有幾個人發出咯咯笑聲。我滿臉通紅走上舞台。卡普太太比了一下，要我走過去站在她身邊。然後她說：「我想我們也應該給這位充滿才藝的年輕人一次熱烈的掌聲，我們的傑克·德瑞克！」她一邊說出我的名字，一邊伸出手拍著我的頭。

我不知道是誰起的頭，但我想應該是班恩·古朗森。因為當孩子們開始鼓掌時，有人開始說著：「傑克·德瑞克、傑克·德瑞克、傑克·德瑞克……」然後禮堂裡的每個孩子都跟著唸了起來。四百個孩子開始唸誦我的名字。

接著發生了一件我所看過最奇怪的事。卡普太太並不像

平常那樣皺起眉頭，要大家停止唸誦，她反而露出笑容開始

拍手，然後跟著孩子們一起唸著：「傑克‧德瑞克、傑克‧

德瑞克、傑克‧德瑞克！」

我不敢相信，感覺自己好像進入了電影，裡面有外星人

占領學校，讓大家的行為變得完全瘋狂。

所有孩子和老師，還有卡普太太，大概唸誦我的名字唸

了十五次，禮堂的屋頂感覺都快被掀翻了。最後，卡普太太

舉起手，喧鬧聲立刻停止。因為即使發生暴動，也沒有人敢

和卡普太太作對。

接著，校長讓我們解散，返回各自的教室準備吃午餐，

就像剛剛完全沒發生過任何怪事一樣。

58

我也試著擺出一副沒事的樣子，眼睛直視地板，走回我們的教室。當某個孩子在走廊上開始唸誦著：「傑克·德瑞克、傑克·德瑞克、傑克·德瑞克！」我並沒有抬頭看，只是繼續前進。

我很高興能夠回到自己的教室。能夠和威利一起坐在某個安靜的角落享用午餐，一定會很棒。

我打開桌子，準備拿出午餐，之後倒抽一口氣。好幾個孩子轉過頭來看我，我的聲音聽起來一定像看到鬼一樣，只不過那東西對我來說比鬼還可怕。因為我完全忘了。那裡，就在我的午餐袋下面，是我曾經看過最可怕的東西——那條亮橘色的巡邏帶！

我沒辦法和我最好的朋友安靜享用午餐了。在短短一小時內，我得再次穿上戲服，走上舞台。這一次，我不再是穿著閃亮盔甲的騎士；這一次，我得戴上鬆垮垮的橘色帶子走進餐廳。因為三、四、五年級的每個孩子都在等我。每個人都在等著垃圾男孩。

危險

4 危險

我想過不要戴著那條橘色巡邏帶吃午餐，大概想了三秒鐘左右，然後我想到卡普太太也會在餐廳。她說過本週接下來的每一天，我都得戴上那個東西。我猜她覺得戴那條帶子應該會感到很光榮，也許就像空手道的黑腰帶一樣。事實上並非如此。

所以我從桌子裡拿出那個東西，掛在一邊的肩膀上，然

後扣在腰部。我抓起午餐，走出教室進到走廊。一群四年級的女生立刻開始對我指指點點，還咯咯笑。但是我把頭抬得高高的，走向餐廳。我繼續走著，並且對自己說：「我撐得過去。我知道我可以。我做得到。」接著假裝沒有任何事情可以影響我。

進到餐廳之後，我開始尋找威利，但他並不在我們平常坐的那張桌子邊。我看到他在排隊拿牛奶，於是走過去跟他說：「嗨！」威利開始像間諜那樣跟我講話，他直直看著前方，試著不讓雙唇移動。

他小聲對我說：「我今天不能和你一起吃。」

我小聲回話：「為什麼？」

危險

他說：「因為卡普太太。她會知道那是我。」

「什麼意思？」我問。

威利說：「我呀。昨天就是我把桌子弄得一團亂的。」

我說：「但我可以告訴她，是我們在玩剪刀、石頭、布，

然後我輸了。」

威利搖搖頭：「呃，最好不要。等會休息時再見。」

威利可能是對的，因為卡普太太已經在餐廳裡四處巡邏

了。

她正在監視有沒有人亂丟垃圾。

於是我拿了牛奶，想找地方坐下來。我環視著餐廳，感

覺每張桌子好像都樹立著一個大標語，標語寫著：禁止老師

的寵物進入。

就連我和威利常坐的那張桌子也擠滿了人。餐廳裡只剩

下一張空桌子，而那張桌子會空著是有原因的，它位在老師

的桌子旁邊。我們學校的老師可以享用免費午餐，其實也不

算真的完全免費。因為如果想吃免費午餐，他們必須和班級

一起在餐廳吃飯。那是卡普太太的主意，她覺得這樣可以讓

餐廳安靜一點。

所以我走向那張空桌子坐下，自己一個人，就只有我和

我的橘色巡邏帶。我對自己說：「我撐得過去。我知道我可

以。我做得到。」

我打開午餐袋，立刻感覺好多了。我媽媽放了巧克力布

丁**外加**無花果夾心派，有兩種點心！這讓我想趕快把其他的

食物解決掉。我才剛咬了一大口波隆納三明治，身後就響起
一個聲音：「這個位置有人坐嗎？今天老師的桌子那邊人太
多了。」

　　是柯特小姐，我的美術老師。我還來不及咀嚼或吞嚥或
吐出一個字，她已經坐在我身邊，並且打開餐盒的蓋子，開
始吃起帶有臭雞蛋和洋蔥味道的沙拉。她就坐在那裡，我的
身邊。當她沒把沙拉塞進自己嘴裡時，就對我微笑，並且聊
天，好像她是我最好的朋友或什麼的。

　　我停止咀嚼，看著餐廳四周。餐廳裡大約有一半的孩子
正盯著我看，盯著我們，我和柯特小姐。我看得出來他們在
想什麼，因為全寫在他們的臉上了，就像葡萄果凍那麼透明

清楚：傑克‧德瑞克真的是老師的寵物，他竟然和老師一起吃午餐！

我很快吃完三明治，然後急忙吃掉我那兩個點心，急到甚至嘗不出味道。然後我看著柯特老師的側臉，說：「我得走了。」她還來不及說任何話，我已經抓起自己的垃圾離開。

我直直走過餐廳，丟掉垃圾，從側門出去，走向運動場。

一走出餐廳外面，我所做的第一件事就是把那條橘色帶子脫掉，塞進口袋。因為卡普太太並沒有規定我在休息時必須戴著它。

威利從運動場的另一邊朝我招手，我跑過去和他會合。

太陽閃閃發亮，天空好藍，小鳥在唱歌。這是個美麗的五月

66

危險

下午，是休息時間。而且我已經撐過午餐了。再一次的，我開始感覺好過多了。

但我還來不及和威利會合，有三個五年級學生突然從立體方格架那裡跳下來追上我。

我停下腳步說：「嗨。」

最大的孩子看起來有點面熟，但我不知道他的名字。他露出惡劣的笑容，然後說：「嗨，垃圾男孩。你最好把你的小帶子穿回去。我想我看到圍欄那邊有些垃圾。」

其中一個戴棒球帽的孩子接著說：「對呀，也許你應該穿上你的假馬，繞著運動場騎馬給我們看。」

他們發出大笑，彼此擊掌，三個人朝著我靠近，並且開

67

始唸誦：「傑克‧德瑞克！傑克‧德瑞克！傑克‧德瑞克！傑克‧德瑞克！傑克‧德瑞克！」他們直逼著我的臉靠近，「傑克‧德瑞克！傑克‧德瑞克！傑克‧德瑞克！」我受不了了。我抓住那個戴棒球帽的傢伙，用盡力氣一推，把他推向另外兩個孩子。他們沒想到我會來這招，三個人全都失去了平衡，一屁股跌坐在草地上，並且停止唸誦我的名字。

他們開始在地上掙扎，努力想爬起來。我看得出是該離開的時候了，於是轉身就跑，卻撞上某個人。是卡普太太，她就站在那裡，看起來好高大，而且很生氣。

「這是在做什麼？你們這些男孩子立刻從地上爬起來！」

那些孩子雖然對我很壞，不過**我**仍然是最先動手的人。

危險

是我開始打架的，所以我說：「卡普太太，我……」

她說：「我知道，傑克。你和這件事情無關。當然沒有關係。」然後她對其他孩子皺起眉頭，「你們這些男孩子，跟我去辦公室。現在。」

那些五年級學生跟在卡普太太身後走，最高大的那個走在最後，他回頭看我，並且瞇起眼睛對我指指點點。我看到他的嘴在動，雖然沒有發出聲音，但我知道他在說什麼。他說：「我會逮到你的！」我不怪他，因為這不公平。是我開啟了這場爭執，但卡普太太沒有看見。

威利走過來說：「好可怕喔！我還以為我們得一次打他們三個呢！」

69

我只能點點頭。一切發生得好快。

威利說：「不過我一點也不想變成現在的你。那個大孩子，你知道他是誰吧，對不對？」

我搖搖頭，然後威利說：「不知道？你**不知道**那是誰？他只不過是全校最凶惡的那是丹尼‧古朗森，班恩的大哥。

孩子，就這樣！」

我站在運動場那裡聽著威利不斷說著有關丹尼‧古朗森的種種，突然很清楚的知道了一件事：身為老師的寵物可能會有危險。非常危險。

5 不再當好好先生

那天下午，在我剛踏上公車的那一秒鐘，後面就有三、四個孩子開始唸誦：「傑克‧德瑞克！傑克‧德瑞克！傑克‧德瑞克！」他們大概可以不停的唸下去，但是公車司機轉過身，要他們閉嘴。

我坐在椅子上，獨自一個人，就像午餐時一樣，只是少了柯特老師。

下了公車之後，我走在回家的路上。獨自一個人。

我沒有心情吃點心，所以上樓進房間。我把門關上，整個人攤平在床上。獨自一個人。

我覺得自己非常可憐。躺在那張床上，我說著每當自怨自憐時會說的話。我說：「不公平！」

確實不公平。我並不想成為老師的寵物，但它就是發生了。我幫斯納文太太解決電腦問題，「砰！」老師的寵物。我上體育課被球轟到，「砰！」老師的寵物。我洗了幾枝筆刷，「砰！」老師的寵物。清理垃圾、不在公車上大吼大叫、幫助說故事的人，「砰！砰！砰！」老師的寵物。

那些老師，甚至是校長，全都覺得我很特別、很棒。

我從床上坐了起來。我有那麼特別、那麼棒嗎？當然沒有！絕對沒有。但是，如果所有的老師都那麼**認為**，他們就會那樣對我。我就會變得**特別**，而且**貼心**，還是個真正的**部隊人**。

這太簡單了。如果我的老師們覺得我總是那麼棒又那麼乖，我只需要去證明他們的看法錯誤。

突然間，我感覺好極了。我跳下床，跑下樓吃點心。我從櫥櫃裡找出一包巧克力碎片餅乾，拿出十片左右堆在盤子上。然後我替自己倒了一大杯牛奶，但牛奶盒裝得很滿，所以我在廚房長桌上灑出不少牛奶。我抓了一張紙巾，開始把牛奶擦掉⋯⋯但接下來，我停止動作。

我露出微笑，把一片餅乾浸到杯子裡，然後壓碎，讓餅乾碎片掉得到處都是。吃完餅乾、把碎片灑了滿桌之後，我把所有的髒亂留在原地，甚至沒把牛奶放回冰箱。然後我對自己說：「好了，如果現在是明天，而我正在學校，我就要直接離開，把東西丟下不管！」

我一邊咧嘴笑著，一邊清理桌面，並且把牛奶盒放回冰箱。那樣的思考是很好的練習。

因為明天我不會當乖小孩，也不會清理自己留下的髒亂。我要變得又壞又粗魯，而且骯髒又討人厭。

因為在星期三，學校裡的每個人都會看到完全不同的傑克‧德瑞克。

6 壞傑克

星期三早上我上公車時，司機看著我爬上階梯。

我經過她身邊，她滿面笑容的對我說：「我最喜歡的公車小乘客今天還好嗎？」

我對著她皺起眉頭，並說：「糟透了。而且公車聞起來很臭！」

那位女士一臉驚嚇，緊抿著嘴把臉轉開，並且抬頭看著

巨大的後照鏡大喊：「快點上來，去後面坐好！」之後，她把門關上，並且抓住方向盤。

我坐了下來，不知道該感覺很糟或是該微笑。但重要的應該是這件事：別再讓這位公車司機覺得傑克・德瑞克是個乖乖牌。我心想：也許她還會因為我太過無禮，把我送進校長的辦公室！那我一定很高興。

因為在那個星期三，我必須變成另一個人，另一個完全不一樣的人。我要惹些麻煩。

下公車時，威利正在等我。我們一起走向運動場，因為還不到進教室的時間。

一個一年級的男孩跑過我們面前，我伸出腳。那孩子被

絆了一下，滾到草地上。

「嘿！」他大喊著，然後站起身說：「那麼做不太好吧！」

我對他做了一個惡劣的表情，然後說：「是嗎？那又怎麼樣？」

那孩子還很小，所以他只是皺起眉頭，繼續往前跑。

威利一臉狐疑的看著我。「你還好嗎？」

我說：「不，一點都不好。所有的老師都覺得我很乖，所有的孩子都覺得我是老師的大寵物。」我停下腳步，看著威利。我說：「他們就是那樣想的，不是嗎？」

威利的臉皺成一團。「嗯……我不太想講啦，不過，對啦。昨天我聽到我們班上有些孩子講到你。他們說，你希望

所有的老師都覺得你很完美。他們說⋯⋯他們說你很噁心。

我⋯⋯我正想告訴他們那不是真的，但那時佛魯太太在看我們，所以我們只好閉上嘴巴。」

我說：「嗯，不用擔心。因為我要來處理這個狀況。就在今天。」

威利一臉疑惑。「什麼意思？」

「我的意思是，我要讓每個人都知道，我才不是老師的寵物，就這樣。」

「但是要怎麼做？」威利問。

「不要那麼乖就好了。」

「你是說，就像⋯⋯就像剛剛把那個孩子絆倒一樣？」威

利問。我點點頭，他說：「可是……如果你那麼做，會惹上麻煩的。」

我看著威利，然後露出微笑，再次點點頭。

接著威利也笑了。「喔……我懂了。」

鐘聲響起，孩子們開始走向門口。

威利說：「嗯，祝你有個很棒的一天。我是說，有個**很壞**的一天！」

我咧嘴笑著說：「**非常壞！**」

進到斯納文太太的教室之後，我把夾克丟到座位下面，然後把背包扔在桌子旁的地板上。

我坐在椅子上，從背包裡拿出一本漫畫書。我從來不曾

在學校裡看過漫畫，感覺相當有趣。

斯納文太太看見我之後，就走到教室後面，坐在離我桌子最近的一部電腦旁。她把電腦打開，弄了一、兩分鐘，然後說：「傑克，這個數學程式又出毛病了。」

我繼續看著我的漫畫，假裝沒聽見。

她繼續敲著鍵盤，然後把手放在膝蓋上，嘆了好大一口氣。「傑克？」我分辨得出來，斯納文太太正在看著我。「傑克，我該怎麼辦？」

我繼續看著我的漫畫說：「去上電腦課。」我就是那樣說的。粗魯、不打算幫忙。而且我的聲音大到教室裡的每個孩子都能聽見。

教室變得非常安靜。我的手在流汗，手指在漫畫書的頁面上留下汗漬。斯納文太太會氣瘋的，我很確定。她已經準備要對我大吼，叫我把正在看的那本垃圾收起來。

五秒鐘過去了。

接著，斯納文太太慢慢站起來，走向我的座位。我感覺得到她站在那裡，有點離我太近。我倒抽一口氣，準備迎接最糟的狀況。她伸出手，準備奪走我的漫畫書。

只是她沒有這麼做。

相反的，她拍拍我的頭。「傑克，你說得一**點也沒錯**！我只是在拖延而已。現在，謝謝你的建議，我決定要這麼做。

我要去報名參加電腦課，就在**今天下午**！因為我如果不會操

作自己教室的電腦，我想我就無權使用它們。所以我們暫時忘了電腦吧。畢竟，誰說一定要用電腦才能學會數線呢？我有好幾疊有關數線的練習題，全都好得不得了。傑克，你真是**太棒了**！我真不知道沒有你該怎麼辦！」

班恩‧古朗森對我擺出一副臭臉，其他大約二十個孩子也是一樣。因為現在我們不能再使用電腦學數學，而是得做練習題。我的意思是，那些數學遊戲雖然相當蠢，但我們至少可以使用電腦，那比練習題要好多了。

接著斯納文太太說：「傑克，你能幫我去一下辦公室，找君克沃特太太拿社區大學的目錄嗎？」

我只是繼續看我的漫畫，並且說：「我正在讀書。」一點

壞傑克

都不乖。我的手還在冒汗。

那麼，斯納文太太怎麼說呢？她是不是說：「年輕人，你給我聽著！立刻放下那本垃圾，去做我叫你做的事！」？

她有沒有抓住我的手說：「我不喜歡你的語氣，德瑞克先生！我們最好到校長室談談這件事！」？

沒有。斯納文太太立刻說：「喔，當然。看我多麼**無禮**。你想在上課之前多讀一點書，我卻一直打斷你。你一向是個**好讀者**。我請別人去。」而且她真的那麼做了。

就在那時候，我決定自己應該再加把勁。我還不夠壞。

點完名並唸完宣誓效忠詞之後，斯納文太太說：「好了，各位同學。在今天的閱讀課，我們要開始討論昨天讀完的故

83

事。嗯，我看看……卡爾，你能說說自己喜歡〈湯姆的寵物烏鴉〉的哪一點嗎？」

卡爾在座位上坐挺了身子，然後說：「嗯，我滿喜歡湯姆教烏鴉如何……」

正當卡爾說話時，我插嘴了。我說：「那個故事我一點都不喜歡。」

斯納文太太揚起眉毛。「一點都不嗎？我的老天，傑克，你不應該打斷卡爾的話……不過，也許你應該告訴我們，你**不喜歡**哪一點？」

我說：「整篇故事都很蠢，而且無聊。我不喜歡它，統統都不喜歡。」

「嗯，」斯納文太太說：「你們其他人呢？還有其他人不喜歡這個故事嗎？」

我看看四周，幾乎每個孩子的手都舉在半空中。然後我想⋯嘿！看！我是領袖耶！他們全都同意我的看法。所以他們應該知道我不是老師的寵物！萬歲！

斯納文太太看看四周，接著看看我，然後深吸一口氣，再慢慢吐出來。我想⋯喔哦，我要遭報應了！

接著她笑了，對著我。而且她說：「傑克，你說得太對了！我也不是那麼喜歡這個故事。經過這一課，我知道必須再多花一些心思注意故事好不好！所以我們跳過這裡吧。把閱讀課本翻到⋯⋯一直翻到第兩百八十七頁。」

當我們翻頁時，斯納文太太說：「好，這是一個比較長的故事，沒辦法在閱讀時間讀完。不過你們可以帶回家，晚上把它讀完。希望你們會比較喜歡這個故事，因為，就像傑克說的，一個故事不應該無聊或愚蠢。好了，現在我要大家拿出一張紙，寫下你覺得可以讓〈湯姆的寵物烏鴉〉變得更好的三種方式。」

教室裡的孩子們全都發出呻吟聲，並對我擺出一張臭臉。因為我們現在必須寫作文，**而且**我們還有回家作業，**而且**那全是我的錯。再加上斯納文太太仍然對我保持微笑，並且說我很聰明。

我開始感到懷疑：**我到底要表現得多壞，她才不會再把**

我當成甜心寶貝？因為使壞，並不像一些孩子所表現的那麼容易。

一會兒後，上美術課時，柯特小姐走過來看我為母親節畫的圖。她在那裡站了一分鐘，然後說：「傑克，那真是太**貼心**了！我想這是我所見過最**貼心**的母親節圖畫！」

上美術課之前，我並不知道要怎麼在柯特小姐的課堂上使壞。但她這麼一說，我立刻知道該怎麼做了。我從圖畫的底部一抓，把圖畫紙從畫架的夾子上扯下來，然後撕掉，說：「嗯，我覺得這張畫爛透了！」我說得很大聲，接著我拿起剛剛使用的小水彩筆，從中折斷。

柯特小姐張著嘴站在那裡。教室裡每個孩子都在看她，

等著她大發雷霆。接著她深吸一口氣，在椅子上坐下。她開始點頭，然後用一種柔和的聲音說：「各位同學，我希望大家注意聽。」其實她根本不需要這麼說。她仍然繼續點著頭。

我覺得她隨時都會開始尖叫。她環視著教室，並且說：「傑克剛剛**非常**勇敢。你們看，我說我喜歡他的畫，而傑克做了什麼？他把畫撕掉。他**知道**他可以畫得更好，而且不害怕把自己的作品撕掉，重新開始！傑克，我覺得你可能是全校最好的美術學生！」接著柯特小姐對我露出笑容，彷彿我剛剛畫出蒙娜麗莎或什麼似的。所以美術課也失敗了。我仍然是老師的寵物。

柯林斯先生有一項重要的規矩，就是「不許盪繩子」，所

以體育課一開始我做了什麼？我去盪了繩子，而且一邊盪一邊大喊：「呀呼！」當柯林斯先生從走廊過來看到我時，他做了什麼？他有過來抓我嗎？他有對我揮舞拳頭嗎？沒有，他張嘴笑了。然後他說：「我一直在猜，誰會是今年第一個打破這條規矩的孩子。我喜歡孩子有點**氣魄**，有點**骨氣**！你們其他孩子可以從傑克·德瑞克身上學到一課。好了，部隊人，從繩子上下來，做五下伏地挺身。下一個盪繩子的孩子得做三十下伏地挺身和三十下仰臥起坐，所以你們其他人別想打什麼主意。」

接著到了午餐時間，我把橘色帶子拿給卡普太太，說：「我不想再戴它了。」我惹上麻煩了嗎？沒有。卡普太太拍拍

我的頭，對著餐廳裡所有的人宣布了一件事。她對著我笑，並且說傑克·德瑞克非常無私。她說，傑克·德瑞克希望讓其他人也能分享戴上午餐巡邏帶的樂趣。接著，她把帶子交給班恩·古朗森。班恩可就沒對我笑了。

下午的數學時間，也沒有任何人對我感到滿意，因為我們全都得寫三張練習題，沒辦法使用電腦。全都是因為我。

所以到了星期三下午放學前，我準備要放棄了。一整天下來，我盡量表現出自己所知最壞、最粗魯的模樣，但完全得不到好處。我仍然是老師的寵物，**所有老師的寵物。**

放學後，我搭上公車，一陣檸檬味襲捲向階梯下的我。

接著我看到司機的椅子背後掛著三包黃色的空氣清香劑。我

還來不及走過司機身旁，她已經抓著我，給我一個大擁抱。

她說：「今天早上聽了你說的話之後，嗯，我立刻去幫公車買了這些東西。我今天去照顧我的小孫子時，他爬上我的腿說：『奶奶今天好香！』你可從沒聽過這麼可愛的話對吧？」然後那位女士再一次擁抱我，並且當著大家的面說：

「你還是我最喜愛的小乘客！」

毫無疑問，我得到一張前往寵物谷的單程車票了。

7 惡夢與好點子

星期三晚上，我作了一個夢。

我在一個籠子裡，一個小小的鐵絲籠，放在室內。我用兩手和雙膝跪立著。籠子裡有兩個碗，一個裝滿喜瑞爾穀片，另一個裝滿沙士。我不時低下頭，吃一大口喜瑞爾，然後舔舔沙士。在我四周全是小籠子，裡面關著其他孩子，其中一個是馬克，還有班恩·古朗森，以及瑪莎、卡爾……甚

至還有威利。我們全都一邊吃著喜瑞爾，一邊舔著汽水。

接著，有一位高大的女士走進房間。她彎下腰，巡視每一個籠子。她看了看瑪莎的籠子，一邊看一邊皺起眉頭說：「不！」然後她看了看班恩，皺著眉頭說：「不！」，她看了每一個籠子，並且不斷說著：「不！不！不！」

接著，她彎腰看著我的籠子，然後微笑了，並且說：「對了！」她打開我的籠子，把橘色的狗項圈套在我的脖子上，並拿出一塊水果夾心派，說：「好孩子！」我坐直身體，她把水果夾心派塞進我的嘴巴。我開始咀嚼水果夾心派，然後這位高大女士彎下腰，拍拍我的頭。她說：「現在，你是我的小寵物了！」我抬頭看著那位女士的臉，是卡普太太！

我從床上坐起來，抓著自己的脖子，開始大喊：「不！不！快把項圈拿掉！我不是你的寵物！不！不要！」

就在那時候，我爸跑進我的房間，打開燈。

「放輕鬆，傑克，沒事了。」爸爸坐在我的床邊，握著我的手臂。「沒事了，傑克。你只是在做夢，沒事的。你是傑克，我是你爸，我們現在在自己的家裡，你已經醒了，一切都沒事了。」我在發抖，而且全身都是汗。爸爸一直握著我的手臂，我很高興他在這裡。

當我完全清醒過來後，爸爸說：「作惡夢啦？嗯？」

我點點頭：「對，可怕的惡夢。」我發著抖，然後說：

「爸，你曾經是老師的寵物嗎？」

他說：「嗯，我想想看……有，我想我曾經是，有過一次，那時我六年級。」

我的眼睛張得好大……「真的？你**想要**那樣嗎？」

爸爸微笑著。「我想要嗎？是的，應該是。我的英文老師是一位女士，叫做帕瑪太太，非常聰明。而且我猜我也覺得她很漂亮。我的朋友提姆和我下課後有時會留下來，幫忙做一點事，像是擦黑板、整理教室之類的事。所以我猜，我們兩個都是老師的寵物。」

我皺著眉。「那她對你和你的朋友很特別嗎？或者，是不是你們犯錯也沒關係？」

爸爸想了一下，然後點點頭。「是的，我想她有，至少有

一點點。我記得有一次我沒有寫作業，被帕瑪太太逮到。她對著我皺眉頭，當著全班的面責罵我，叫我放學後去找她。但是我放學後去找她的時候，她只是笑了笑，並且說：『好了，以後不可以再這樣了。你還會嗎，吉米？』我說：『不會的。』接著她就讓我離開了。在那之後，我也真的每次都會寫作業。」

「但其他孩子呢？」我問：「他們不會因為你是老師的寵物而討厭你嗎？」

爸爸抓抓頭，原本就亂的頭髮變得更亂了。他說：「我不太記得了。我只記得帕瑪太太有時會經常對我微笑。」

我說：「但如果你有很多老師，而他們全都對你超級好，

雖然你甚至不喜歡他們微笑的方式，然後所有的孩子都覺得你是故意做個乖乖牌。那怎麼辦？」

「嗯⋯⋯」接著爸爸打了一個好大的呵欠。「如果我是**故意**要從老師那裡得到特別的待遇，那麼我猜那些孩子的想法並沒有錯。因為那就像我做了什麼，而想要脫罪一樣。但如果是老師自己決定要對你比對其他的孩子好，那就不是你的錯，而是老師的錯。因為做老師的，不應該對某個孩子比較好，對不對？」

我點點頭，然後爸爸說：「現在聽著。你躺回枕頭上，把眼睛閉起來，回去睡覺，好嗎？」他幫我把被子蓋到下巴下面，親親我的臉，然後起身，把燈關上。「晚安，傑克。」

「晚安，爸。」

「好好睡。」

然後，我又是獨自一個人了。我繼續想著，因為爸爸說得對，做老師的，不應該對某個孩子比較好；校長也不該那麼做。而且我並沒有故意要成為老師的寵物，我只是做我自己而已，所以那不是我的錯。甚至當我故意表現得很壞，也沒有用，因為……因為我就是不壞，而且大家都知道。

接著，我想到一個很大的點子。很大，而且很單純。但會有效嗎？也許這個想法太單純了。

想找出答案只有一個辦法，而且只能去一個地方找，那就是學校，在星期四。所以現在第一件事是要回去睡覺，我

就那麼做了。
而且我不再夢到有關橘色狗項圈的事。

8 沒那麼特別

嘗試一項新計畫或許很嚇人，但如果不去嘗試，就沒辦法知道計畫會不會成功。

所以星期四一早，就在點完名、唸完效忠誓詞且老師宣布過注意事項之後，我舉起手，等著斯納文太太叫我。

她說：「是的，傑克？」

我深吸一口氣，然後說：「斯納文太太，你知道自己對

電腦有多麼傷腦筋吧？嗯，我想，如果我們今天想用電腦學數學，那你真的應該問問雪莉，她對電腦的了解比我多太多了。還有班恩，他對程式很在行。他們能提供真正的幫助。

那麼，就算你的電腦課還沒上完，我們也許還是可以用電腦學數學。因為比起練習題，用電腦有趣多了。」

斯納文太太說：「也許閱讀時間之後會有時間試試看。

大家覺得這樣好嗎？」

班上許多孩子都點頭說：「好。」

然後斯納文太太說：「那是個好主意，傑克。謝謝你。」

她對我微笑。

而我根本不在意她是否對我微笑，因為那**的確**是個好主

意。我也不在乎全班同學是不是看到她在對我笑，因為，為了一個好主意而感到開心，並沒有什麼不對，是吧？再說，分享一個好主意並不會讓我成為老師的寵物，對吧？那只會讓我做自己。

那是我前一晚想出來的大創意。做我自己，而不去在乎自己是不是老師的寵物。因為，如果我知道我**不是**老師的寵物，那我就不是，對吧？

但這有點難處理。因為如果你得到特殊的待遇，每個人還是會把你當作老師的寵物。當某個孩子得到特別待遇，其他孩子就會討厭。因為那不公平，而且真的不公平，因為老師理當用同樣的方式對待所有孩子。

閱讀時間之後，斯納文太太需要一個人幫忙把午餐的費用送到辦公室。我問她能不能讓我去，但不是因為我想成為老師的寵物。我要去辦公室有別的原因。

當我到辦公室後，我把錢交給學校祕書，然後說：「卡普太太在忙嗎？」

君克沃特太太從櫃台後面看著我，她說：「是的，傑克。請在那裡坐著等一下。」

所以我坐下來，深吸一口氣。就算沒惹麻煩，等著見校長還是不好玩。

幾分鐘之後，卡普太太出來了。她一看到我就露出滿臉笑容，並說：「進來我的辦公室，傑克。」我進去之後，她坐

了下來，我很高興她這麼做。在坐下之前，卡普太太顯得非

常高大，特別嚇人。接著她問：「好了，有什麼事需要我幫

忙嗎？」

我再次深吸一口氣，然後說：「我遇到一個問題。從星

期一開始，許多事情發生在我身上，那些事讓其他孩子都覺

得我是老師的大寵物。」

接著我停下來觀察她的表情。我想確定她看起來並沒有

在生氣或怎樣。她沒有，於是我繼續說下去：「因為，我並

不是老師的寵物。我只是一個普通的小孩。但如果大家都覺

得我是，那就糟了，對吧？」

卡普太太緩緩點頭說：「是⋯⋯我了解那會是個問題，

而且老師不該給孩子特權。有些老師對你比較特別嗎？」

我說：「嗯，有點。有時候。我覺得啦。」

卡普太太坐在椅子上的身體向前一傾，然後她說：「真的？什麼時候？是誰？」

我特別用力的深呼吸一口氣，然後說：「像在星期二。是……是你。」

「什麼？你在說什麼？」卡普太太看起來有點生氣，但我的話不能只說一半。

所以我告訴她，那天我怎麼在運動場那裡開啟爭端，又怎麼推倒那個五年級的學生，以及那些孩子怎樣惹上了麻煩，而我卻沒事。因為她說她知道那不是我的錯，事實上卻是。

卡普太太的身體靠回椅背上，她把指尖貼在一起。「啊，是，我了解那會是個問題，雖然我並沒有看見你推任何人。在那之前，是集會……然後是餐廳的事。我的老天！這個星期對你來說可真是不容易，是吧，傑克？」

我點點頭說：「是，真的是這樣。」

卡普太太站起來，繞過桌子。「嗯，你最好回去教室了，傑克。這件事我會想一想。也許午餐時我們再多談一會兒。」

「午餐嗎？」我問：「那時我再過來辦公室這裡嗎？」

卡普太太沉默了一下，然後她說：「不用。我會去找你，好嗎？我很高興你這麼勇敢，過來找我談。」

我感覺得出來，卡普太太想要拍拍我的頭。但她沒有，

我很高興。

回到教室之後，已經是自由活動的時間，有些孩子在讀書，有些在畫畫或是玩樂高積木，而雪莉和班恩正在電腦前工作。

我走回去，站在班恩身邊，從他肩膀後面看向螢幕。當他看到我時，我問：「修好了嗎？」

他仍然看著電腦螢幕。「對呀，很簡單。但我假裝很難，這樣我才可能在午餐時進來，然後就可以玩遊戲了。」班恩的手從鍵盤上離開，伸入口袋。他轉頭確認斯納文太太沒有在看，然後拿出一片光碟讓我看一眼，是「坦克大戰」。「我都隨身帶著這個備分，以防萬一會用到。」他咧嘴一笑。

那天是星期四，沒有美術課或體育課。自由活動之後，我們在社會課看了一部影片，是路易斯和克拉克這兩位冒險家的故事。看起來就像長篇冒險故事，只不過內容是真的。

那天早上過得很不錯，其中最棒的部分是，我感覺得出來，班上的孩子不再把我當成老師的寵物了。

但我從教室走出走廊準備去吃午餐時，佛魯太太班上的一些孩子看到我，其中一個男生說：「嘿，看！是傑克‧德克克呢！今天要和你的女朋友柯特小姐一起吃午餐嗎？」

接著有三、四個五年級的孩子開始說：「傑克‧德瑞克！傑克‧德瑞克！傑克‧德瑞克！」其中一個還把我的午餐打到地上，一顆蘋果從袋子裡滾了出來。

我想要揍人，但我沒有。我撿起午餐，走向餐廳，一邊想著：也許在我自己的班上情況變好了，但其他孩子呢？其他老師呢？

我感覺學校裡的其他人，在接下來的日子裡，還是會一直把我當成老師的寵物。

9 還算安全的緊急降落

餐廳裡的情況也沒有改善。排隊拿牛奶時，一個四年級的學生問我怎麼還沒去清理桌子。接著一個五年級孩子說：

「嘿，看！是原版的垃圾男孩耶！」

當我走往威利坐著的那張桌子時，佛魯太太班上的一個女生說：「嘿，傑克……柯特小姐今天上美術課時一直提到你。她說你真是太**貼心**了！」然後一整群女生開始咯咯笑。

111

我是傑克，完美馬屁精

我坐下來，把巧克力牛奶丟給威利。我說：「嗨！所以你覺得今天和我坐在一起還算安全嗎？」

「是呀，我想應該是吧。看起來你還是很有名。」

我點點頭，一口咬下我的花生醬三明治。「對。我猜我得學會這樣活下去。」

我仰起頭，準備喝一大口牛奶，但又停住。威利不大對勁，是他的臉。威利看起來就好像電影《侏羅紀公園》裡那兩個看到暴龍正要吃掉他們車子的孩子。我放下牛奶，並說：「有什麼不對嗎？」

威利悄悄說著：「卡普太太朝這邊來了，走得很快。」

我轉身一看，威利並不是在開玩笑。卡普太太正穿過餐

112

廳走來，每個孩子都在看她。她帶著一臉可怕的表情，而且走得很快，正筆直的朝我們靠近。

她直直走向我。我感覺得到自己的臉變得慘白，心臟怦怦跳。卡普太太低頭瞪著我。她好高，一張臉像是用石頭做的一樣。

她一句話也沒說，伸出手一把抓住我手肘上方的手臂。

接著，她用響亮的聲音說：「你和我去辦公室。現在！」

威利看起來一副想鑽進桌底下的模樣。

然後卡普太太轉身開始向前走。她還是抓著我的手臂，似乎打算把我拖過餐廳。一路上經過的每個人都盯著我看。

卡普太太用她的大嗓門說：「我們有事要談一談，年輕人。

關於體育課的**繩子**，以及你在美術教室的**行為**，還有星期二在**運動場**發生的事。」我抬起頭，看到丹尼·古朗森正在一張午餐桌旁。他一邊點頭一邊對我笑，接著伸出食指，**刷！**朝著脖子橫畫一下。

卡普太太拖著我走過那間大餐廳，我感覺自己開始臉紅。我想：「我再也不相信任何校長了。我自以為很聰明，去找她談，現在她大概還會打電話給我爸媽。」

然後我們走出門口，下了樓梯，沿著前方走廊，進入她的辦公室。

我覺得自己快哭了，我討厭這樣，尤其是在學校。但那正是我的感覺。我只能一直盯著地板。等我在卡普太太桌前

115

椅子上坐下，並聽到她坐上她的位子時，我才抬頭看她。

然後，我很快把視線轉開，接著又看了一眼，因為我不敢相信我的眼睛。卡普太太在笑，她的臉上掛著一個又大又溫暖的和善笑容。

我繼續盯著她，她說：「怎麼樣？」

我搖搖頭。「什麼？什麼怎麼樣？」

「我的表演啊。你還喜歡我的演出嗎？」卡普太太繼續笑著說：「如果能騙過你，那我猜我的表演應該相當不錯。抱歉，但是我必須讓它看起來像真的一樣。」

我搖著頭，還在努力試著理解。「那麼，你沒有……生我的氣？」

她搖搖頭，還是在笑。「沒有，完全沒有。還記得今天早上我說過，我要想一想你的⋯⋯問題嗎？嗯，我想了。而剛剛發生的事，就是我的解決辦法。」

那時我才終於了解這全是一場戲。我說：「但體育課的繩子呢？我真的做了。」

卡普太太說：「我和柯林斯先生談過，他了解狀況。所以你明天將要多做一些伏地挺身和仰臥起坐。」

「那美術課呢？」我問。

「是的，柯特小姐星期五會好好教訓你一頓，讓你知道損毀學校公物是不對的行為。當然，那是實話，你不應該折斷那枝水彩筆的。」

接著卡普太太看看她的手錶。「嗯，我想你現在回去把午餐吃完，應該已經很安全了。不過要記得，傑克，這件事必須保密，否則看起來會像是我給你的**特殊待遇**，而我們現在都不想要任何人**那麼**想，對吧？」

就在那個時候，即使卡普太太想要拍拍我的頭，我也完全不介意了。

於是我生命中最長的四天總算結束了。我從不曾把卡普太太那場精采的演出告訴任何人，甚至連威利也不知道。

那個星期四剩下的午餐，吃起來非常美味。當我走回餐廳坐下來吃飯時，每個人看我的那種方式，真希望也能讓你

們看看。

　有些孩子看我的樣子，好像我是一個逃犯。有些孩子看我的樣子，像在看一個從戰場上回來的英雄。有些孩子看我的樣子，就像他們根本不敢看我。但是沒有任何人看我的樣子（包括所有孩子、老師、餐廳阿姨），好像我**曾經**是「老師的寵物」，傑克‧德瑞克。

安德魯·克萊門斯 ⑭

Jake Drake
TEACHER'S PET

ANDREW CLEMENTS

Contents

CHAPTER ONE

Four Bad Days

I'm Jake—Jake Drake. I'm right in the middle of fourth grade. One thing I like about fourth grade is that I'm not in kindergarten, first grade, second grade, or third grade anymore. And I'm not at Miss Lulu's Dainty Diaper Day Care anymore either.

I think fourth grade is my best grade so far. It's so good that I have to think hard to

remember anything about it that's bad at all. Like right now? I can only think of one day that wasn't so great. That was the day I thought my teacher Mr. Thompson was being unfair.

It was because of the way he treated Shawn Underwood that day. First of all, Mr. Thompson picked Shawn to lead the Pledge of Allegiance. Then Mr. Thompson let Shawn take the attendance sheets to the office. During math, Mr. Thompson asked Shawn to write the answer on the chalkboard. After morning recess, Mr. Thompson let Shawn pick out the new chapter book for class read-aloud time. And then Mr. Thompson picked Shawn to line up first for lunch.

I know it sounds like I'm making too big a deal out of these things. But it was like Shawn was Mr. Thompson's favorite. It was like Shawn

was the teacher's pet. And that's not fair.

Turns out I was wrong about Shawn, though. After lunch that day, Mr. Thompson said, "I have some good news, and some bad news. The good news is that at the end of the day we're going to have a party with cake and ice cream. But the bad news is that it's a going-away party for Shawn. Tomorrow Shawn is moving to another state, and we're all going to miss him a lot."

Mr. Thompson was being extra nice to Shawn because it was his last day. So Shawn wasn't really the teacher's pet. And I was glad because I liked Shawn, and being the teacher's pet is one of the worst things that can happen to a kid at school.

You know what stinks about being a teacher's pet? Everything, that's what.

I know this for sure because of what happened

last May, right near the end of third grade. It all happened in four days—less than a week. But to me, those four days felt like four years. Because for those four days, I was in great danger.

I was in danger of losing my friends. I was in danger of losing my reputation. I was in danger of losing...my mind.

Because that was the time I became Jake Drake, Teacher's Pet.

When I was in third grade, we got five new computers in our classroom. Mrs. Snavin was my third-grade teacher, and she acted like computers were scary, especially the new ones. She always needed to look at a how-to book and the computer at the same time. Even then, she got mixed up a lot. Then she had to call Mrs.

Reed, the librarian, to come and show her what to do.

So it was a Monday morning in May, and Mrs. Snavin was sitting in front of a new computer at the back of the room. She was confused about a program we were supposed to use for a math project. My desk was near the computers, and I was watching her.

Mrs. Snavin looked at the screen, and then she looked at this book, and then back at the screen again. Then she shook her head and let out this big sigh. I could tell she was almost ready to call Mrs. Reed.

I've always liked computers, and I know how to do some stuff with them. Like turn them on and open programs, play games and type, make drawings, and build Web pages—things like that. So I got up from my desk, pointed at

the screen, and said, "Mrs. Snavin, if you double-click on that little thing right there, then the program will start running. And then you click on this, and that opens up the part about number lines."

So Mrs. Snavin did what I told her to and the program started running. Because that's the way it works and anybody knows that. Except Mrs. Snavin.

When the program started playing this stupid music, Mrs. Snavin smiled this huge smile at me and said, "Jake, you're *wonderful!*" And she said it too loud. *Way* too loud.

She said it so loud that every kid in the classroom stopped and turned to look at us, just in time to see Mrs. Snavin pat me on the top of my head like I was a nice little poodle or something. An embarrassed poodle with a

bright red face.

So I mumbled something like, "Oh, it was nothing." Which was a mistake.

Because right away she said, "But you're wrong, Jake. I get so mixed up when I work with these new computers. And to think that all along I've had such a *wonderful* expert right here in my classroom, and I didn't even know it! From now on you're going to be my special computer helper!"

I sat down fast before she could pat me on the head again. But the worst part hadn't happened yet. Because Mrs. Snavin walked to the front of the room and said, "Class, if any of you has trouble with the computers during math time this afternoon, just ask Jake what to do. He's my *special* computer helper!"

By this time, my face was so red that I felt

my ears start to get hot. I kept my eyes on my desk but even so, I knew everyone in the room was looking at me. And I was just waiting for someone to start making fun of me, especially the kids who know tons more about computers than I do. Like Ben. Or Shelly Orcut. She's the biggest computer brain in our whole school.

But just then the first period bell rang and it was time to go to art class. So I was saved by the bell.

Miss Cott's room was a big mess that morning. That's probably why I've always liked the art room so much. It's the one place at school where you don't have to worry about neatness. Or spilling stuff. Or getting everything done in a hurry.

The first thing we did in art class was put on our giant shirts. They're supposed to keep

paint and glue and junk off our clothes. I put on an old blue shirt of my dad's. The other kids put on their giant shirts too, so we all looked like our legs had shrunk. Which is another fun thing about art class.

So on that Monday I went to work at an easel near the windows. We were supposed to be making pictures for Mother's Day.

I was about half done with my painting when I decided I needed a smaller brush. So I went to the big sink to get one. About fifteen or twenty brushes were sticking out of a bucket full of brownish greenish yellowish water. I grabbed a handful of brushes and looked for one that was the right size. Then I felt someone come up behind me. So I hurried up and rinsed off all the brushes under the faucet, took the one I wanted, and stuck the rest on the rack

above the sink.

I looked behind me, and Miss Cott was standing there. She had this goofy look on her face, and her head was tilted to one side, and she was smiling. At me.

"Jake! That is the *sweetest* thing anybody has done in this room all week!" Which didn't make sense since it was only Monday morning and there hadn't been much of a week yet. But I guess that didn't matter to Miss Cott.

I gave this lame little smile and said, "I...I need a smaller brush so I can finish..."

Miss Cott said, "And instead of working to finish your picture, you've stopped to help clean up the brushes! That is so *sweet*!" By then, the whole class was watching us, and I was wishing that Miss Cott would stop saying "*sweet*" like that.

But Miss Cott wasn't done. She turned to all the kids in my class and said, "If all of you would be as *sweet* as Jake is and help clean up a little, then maybe this room wouldn't be such a mess all the time. Thank you *so much*, Jake!"

And as she said that, Miss Cott patted me on the head.

I took my small brush and hurried back to my easel. I started working on my picture again, trying not to feel so embarrassed.

Then I heard Ben whisper something to Mark. In addition to being great with computers, Ben Grumson was probably the meanest kid in my third-grade class. So he whispered extra loud so I'd be sure to hear him. "Hey, Mark, don't you think Jake is just about perfect? He's so *sweet*!" I pretended not to hear, but I know my face turned redder and redder.

After art, we went back to our classroom for reading and social studies, and nothing much happened.

Then right before lunch, we had gym class. Mr. Collins was having one of his tough-guy days. You can tell when Mr. Collins is having a tough-guy day because on tough-guy days, he calls all the boys and girls "troops."

After the bell rang, Mr. Collins blew his whistle and shouted, "Okay, troops, listen up. Get in a straight line here at the middle of the court. Come on, troops, look alive! Today we're going to play...dodgeball!"

Half the class groaned, and the other half cheered. The kids who always get whomped by that fat, red ball groaned, and the kids who are great at throwing and catching cheered. I was one of the kids who groaned. For me, dodgeball

means trying to stay alive.

Mr. Collins clapped his hands. "All right, troops! Everyone whose last name starts with A through L, over to the far side of the court. M through Z, over here behind me. Let's hustle! Go, go, go!"

Mr. Collins started the game by rolling the ball along the black line down the middle of the gym. Glen Purdy ran out and grabbed the ball for the other team.

There's something...weird about dodgeball. I don't know why it brings out the worst in some kids, but it does. Take Glen Purdy, for example. In real life, Glen is a pretty good kid. He's friendly, he's a good partner in math or reading, and he's good to have on your side in a basketball game because he's so tall.

But when a game of dodgeball starts up, all

of a sudden this nice guy turns into a beast. And his arms are so long that when Glen throws that fat, red ball, it's like it was shot from a cannon.

So Glen had the ball, and right away, our whole team backed all the way against the wall. We knew that Glen was going to whomp someone. And he did.

Me. Right on the shoulder.

It took only about four minutes for the rest of my team to get knocked out, and then Mr. Collins clapped his hands and said, "Let's go troops, another round, and this time it's a two-ball game."

And he rolled both balls along the black center line.

Which meant that now it was possible for some kid to get whomped with *two* fat, red balls

at the same time. And that's what happened. To me. On the first throw. Again. I got one ball on the ankle and one ball in the stomach.

Here's what the next four games of dodgeball were like for me that day: *WHOMP! WHOMP! WHOMP! WHOMP!* Six games of dodgeball, and I was the first kid to get knocked out in every one of them.

But did I ask if I could go to the nurse when the third *WHOMP* knocked me down and I skinned my knee? No. And did I ask if I could lie down on the mats when the fifth *WHOMP* got me right on the head and made me see little rainbows all over the place? No. How come? Maybe because I was being stupid. But it's probably because I'm not that big so even if I get hurt sometimes, I don't want anybody to think I'm a quitter.

Anyway, I was so glad when that gym class was finally over that I was the first in line at the door to be dismissed for lunch.

Mr. Collins came over to the doorway. He gave a blast on his whistle to quiet everyone down. Then he said, "Listen up, troops. You all played great today. Good job. But the player of the Day, maybe the Player of the Month Award goes to a special guy. Did everyone see who took the first hit in every game today? Did that person complain? No. Did he whine and groan? No. Why? Because he's a real trooper, that's why. Jake Drake here deserves my Gym Class Medal of Honor, and you can all take some lessons from him on how to be a good sport. All right, troops—dismissed!"

And of course, as Mr. Collins was talking about me, what was he doing? He was patting

me on the head. And as he was talking, I was looking at the other kids, and I could tell they didn't think I should be getting all this attention just because I stink at dodgeball.

Standing there at the door of the gym with Mr. Collins patting me on the head, I got this sinking feeling in the pit of my stomach.

Because Monday was only half over, and I was already well on my way to becoming the most unpopular kid in the history of Despres Elementary School.

CHAPTER TWO

Garbage Guy

I went to my classroom after gym to grab my lunch bag, and then I hurried to the cafeteria. I wanted to sit with Willie. He's my best friend. His real name is Phil but his last name is Willis, so everyone calls him Willie. He was in Mrs. Frule's class when we were in third grade, so I only got to see him at lunch and at recess.

"Hi, Willie." I put my lunch on the table,

and then went to get in the milk line.

Standing there, I looked over at a table and saw two girls from my class, Marsha and Jane. Marsha was looking at me and whispering something to Jane. Then Jane looked at me, then they looked at each other, and then they both started laughing. I didn't like them laughing that way, but there was nothing I could do about it, so I got milk for Willie and me and went to sit down.

As I was walking back to my seat, I had to go past Ben Grumson. He was standing at the end of the lunch line with Karl Burton. And when I went past Ben, he grinned at Karl and said, "Hey, look, it's Jake. He's a real *trooper*; y'know. And *sweet*, too." Karl laughed, even though he's one of my friends. I don't blame him. I guess it *was* pretty funny. Except not to

me, not at that moment. I just gritted my teeth and walked back to Willie's table.

Willie nodded toward Ben and said, "What was that about?"

"That?" I said, "Nothing much. I got hit out first in dodgeball six times in a row in gym today. And then Mr. Collins made a big deal about it. So Ben was teasing me."

Willie made a face. "How can you stand being in Ben's class? He's such a jerk."

"Yeah," I agreed, "he is."

But then we started talking about this computer game we wanted to get so we could link up our computers at home and play against each other. So lunch was great because Willie is always fun to talk to, and because I didn't have to worry about getting whomped on the side of the head by a fat, red ball.

When our cookies were gone, I said, "Let's go." With me and Willie, that meant it was time to play Rock, Paper, Scissors. Because every day after lunch we play three games of Rock, Paper, Scissors to see who has to carry our garbage to the trash barrel.

I won the first game, but Willie won the next two. He smiled and said, "I have to take a book back to the library, so maybe I'll see you after school."

I started to clean up. Willie is not what you would call a neat eater. His orange peels were all over the place, and he had flipped some potato chips around when he popped the bag open. Plus he had spilled some chocolate milk.

So I was standing up, leaning across the table, wiping up milk some napkins, when all of a sudden, right behind me, I heard the sound

that scares the daylights out of every kid at Despres Elementary School.

"YOU THERE!"

My heart just about jumped out of my mouth. Because only one person at my school has a voice like that, and that's Mrs. Karp, the principal.

"Stop that, put that stuff down, and stand up straight!" Mrs. Karp was almost yelling, so the whole cafeteria got completely quiet. She has the kind of voice that makes kindergartners cry. It's so loud that I think she could break windows if she really shouted.

Mrs. Karp came over and stood right next to me. She looked around to make sure that everyone in the cafeteria was paying attention, and then with her huge voice said, "Every day, our cafeteria helpers have to spend extra time

after lunch cleaning up in here. Take a good look at this table." She pointed at the mess in front of me—two ripped-up lunch bags, a squished chocolate-milk carton, three bent straws, a wad of soggy napkins, and a pile of orange peels and potato chips. It was not a pretty picture. I gulped, frozen with fear. Then Mrs. Karp said, "Jake Drake has not only started to clean up his own things, but he was also cleaning up the mess left behind by some *bad* citizen."

I looked up, and over by the door I saw Willie standing there—Willie the bad citizen. He made this scared face at me, like maybe he thought I was going to point at him and say, *There he is! He's the table trasher!* But I would never do that.

Mrs. Karp had something in her hand. It was one of those patrol belts, the kind crossing

guards wear. She leaned over toward me, and before I could do anything, she looped the strap over my head, pulled the belt around my waist, and hooked it together. It was way too big for me, so it sagged all over. Then she smiled and said, "See this patrol belt?" Which was a stupid question, because the thing is bright orange. It's impossible *not* to see it. "This week we're all going to make a special effort to keep our lunchroom clean. Jake Drake is going to wear this belt during lunch for the rest of the week. That will help to remind all of us not to leave *any* trash on our tables. And I want everyone to give Jake a nice round of applause for being such a fine lunchroom citizen. Jake, you've set a good example for everyone!"

And then Mrs. Karp started clapping and looking around the cafeteria, so everyone else

had to clap too. And I saw Willie, over in the doorway, clapping like mad and grinning at me.

And once everyone was clapping, what did Mrs. Karp do? She stopped clapping, she reached over, and with all the kids in the third, fourth, and fifth grades watching, she patted me on the head.

The clapping ended, and after she smiled at me once more, Mrs. Karp walked away. I finished cleaning up the lunch table, and tired not to feel like everyone was looking at me. Which is not easy when you're wearing a big, floppy, orange patrol belt. I got out of the cafeteria fast.

Willie was waiting for me in the hallway. He pointed at the orange belt and pretended like it was something amazing. He opened his

eyes up real wide and said, "Gee! Can I touch that?"

I didn't smile. I walked past him because I had to get back to Mrs. Snavin's room fast so I could take off the stupid thing and stick it inside my desk.

Willie caught up and said, "Don't get mad, Jake, I'm just kidding."

"Well, it's not funny," I said. I didn't like what was happening.

When lunch period was over, all the kids in my class went back to our room and we sat down and got out our math workbooks. Mrs. Snavin waited until all the kids got quiet and sat in their seats. Then she said, "Before we start on math, I need someone to take this note down to the office for me."

Right away, about six kids put up their

hands, because some kids love to do that kind of stuff. Mrs. Snavin looked right past all those waving hands. She looked right at me and she smiled and said, "I think I'll have Jake take it." She held out the note toward me, so I had to get up from my seat, walk to the front of the room, and get it from her. Then Mrs. Snavin said, "But be sure to hurry right back, Jake, because we're going to work on our number-line project, and you have to be my *special* computer helper, okay?" And I could feel every kid in the class looking at me. They weren't saying anything. They weren't even whispering. But right then, I heard what they were thinking anyway. They were thinking, *teacher's pet.*

And Mrs. Snavin didn't help. All during the last two hours of the day, she kept asking me to remind her how to do different things on the

computer or to go over and help this kid and then help that kid. And the worst part was that nobody really needed help and they didn't want help, especially from the *teacher's pet*. And Mrs. Snavin came and watched me when it was my turn to use the computer, and she said, "It's so wonderful to see a real *expert* use this math program!" I thought the day would never end.

But it did. When I finally ran outside to wait for my bus, I was in a pretty bad mood. And when I was standing in line, a fifth-grade boy went by and said, "Hey, Garbage Guy! I think Mrs. Karp is in love with you!"

And then all his friends laughed and another kid said, "Yeah—Garbage Guy! Maybe you can clean up *my* lunch table tomorrow. And do a good job, because you don't want to make the principal unhappy!"

Bus number three came and I got on. I sat on the outside edge of a seat so no one could sit with me. I didn't want to talk to anyone. I just sat there, staring at the dirty black floor. All around me kids were talking and joking, yelling and laughing. Not me.

I felt terrible. It wasn't fair. I didn't want to be a teacher's pet. I didn't try to get anybody's s attention. It wasn't my fault. I felt like I was trapped.

I looked up and my stop was next. When the bus stopped, I jumped up and got to the front of the bus. I wanted to be the first one off. I was ready for this day to be over.

It was real noisy, and the lady driving the bus turned around in her seat and shouted, "Quiet!"

When everybody stopped yelling and talking,

the driver looked around and said, "You kids have got to settle down! It's not safe to drive when it gets so loud and crazy. You should all be sitting still in your seats, and if you talk at all, you talk quietly, understand? On this whole bus, only one kid has been a good bus rider today—and that's this kid right here."

And with all the kids on the bus watching her, the bus driver reached over and patted me on the head.

CHAPTER THREE

Special Treatment

When I got home that afternoon, I walked right up to my room. I didn't even get a snack.

That's how come my mom followed me. She came into my room and said, "Jake, is everything all right?"

I didn't know how to explain. Because if I said to her, "All of my teachers, and even the principal, all think I'm wonderful," then my

mom would say something like, "Well, you *are* wonderful, Jake!" Because that's what moms do.

So I said, "I'm okay, Mom. I just got kind of tired at school today." Which was true. Having every kid in the school think you're trying to be the teacher's pet makes you tired. And being whomped six or seven times by a dodgeball doesn't help either.

But after dinner we got to watch this really good TV show about the Coast Guard, and so I stopped thinking about school and I felt better.

After Dad read a chapter of our book at bedtime, and after he tucked me in and kissed me good night and turned out my light, I couldn't help thinking about school again. The way I finally got to sleep was by telling myself it was probably just a bad Monday. I told myself

that tomorrow, everything would go back to normal. Tomorrow, I would just be a regular kid again. That's what I told myself, and I hoped it would be true. I wanted it to be true. I needed it to be true. And I went to sleep believing it.

Tuesday's bus ride to school was great. I was just a kid. Not too loud, not too quiet. The bus driver didn't even notice I was there, and no one said a word about anything that had happened on Monday. And I said to myself, *See? Nothing to worry about.*

But I spoke too soon. The second I walked into her room, Mrs. Snavin said, "Oh, good! You're here, Jake. I don't know how I'll ever survive another day without my *special* computer helper!" Then she pointed at her computer screen and said, "I've got that math program

open, and I'm afraid it's all muddle again. Would you come over here and see if I've done this right?" she hadn't done it right, so I had to fix it for her. And when I was done, Mrs. Snavin said, "Jake, you've saved my life again!"

By that time, almost all the other kids were in the classroom. I could feel them looking at me, and I could tell they were thinking, *There's the teacher's pet, already hard at work.*

And it really looked that way. Because who did Mrs. Snavin pick to take the attendance sheet down to the office? Me. And during reading period, who did Mrs. Snavin call on first to read out loud? Me. And who did Mrs. Snavin choose to be first in line to go to an assembly in the auditorium? Me.

Everyone had been looking forward to that assembly for a while. It was this lady who called

herself Miss Thumbelina the Storyteller. She had performed at our school before, and she was great. She told stories, but she didn't just read them. She acted out all the parts all by herself. She had a bunch of different costumes and hats and beards and wigs, and huge baskets full of things like swords and ropes and lanterns. If there was a castle in a story, then she'd pull a chunk of a castle wall out of basket and make you believe the whole castle was right there.

I was glad Miss Thumbelina was performing that Tuesday. It was only ten-thirty, but already I needed a break. I wanted to sit in a huge room in the middle of all the kids from grades three, four, and five. Then the auditorium would get dark, and I could disappear into the crowd and enjoy the show.

Miss Thumbelina came onto the stage and

we all started clapping. She had on this wig with long red hair. She made a low bow, and then she said, "Good morning! I'm going to start our program today with an old, old story. To help me tell this story, I need a helper, someone who's loyal and true and honest and good, a real knight in shining armor." And then she held one hand up to her forehead to shade her eyes from the bright lights, and with her other hand she pointed our into the audience.

And she pointed at a fourth grader sitting right in front of me. "You there!" she said. "You look like a prince to me! Come on up onstage and help me tell this tale!" The kid started to shake his head no, and I felt sorry for him.

Suddenly Mrs. Snavin was there next to me. She said, "Jake! You're the *perfect* one to help her!" And she said it way too loud. She

grabbed me by the arm and pulled me up out of my seat. When Miss Thumbelina saw me standing up, she clapped her hands and said, "Great! Here comes our prince!"

Fifteen seconds later I was walking across the stage, blinking like crazy and trying not to trip on the stuff that was everywhere.

There's no way to get ready for the worst ten minutes of your life. One minute I was sitting in the dark enjoying the show, and the next minute, I *was* the show, and this lady in a big wig was sticking a knight's helmet on my head and strapping plastic armor around my chest. Then she handed me a long sword, which would have been fun to mess with if four hundred kids hadn't been laughing at me.

Then Miss Thumbelina put this thing around me that was supposed to be a horse.

There was a horse's head in front and a horse's rump and tail in back, and there was a place for me in the middle. The whole thing hung from my shoulders by two straps. To make the horse go, I had to run like this: *ba-da bum, ba-da bum, ba-da bum.*

As she hooked me into the horse, she said, "Now, here's all you have to do: Wait behind the curtains, and whenever I say, 'Someone will save me!' , you come galloping all the way across the stage, right past me. And you wave your sword and yell, 'I'll save you, Princess!' Then you go behind the curtains on the far side and wait there. And when I say that line again, you run out and do the same thing, okay?"

I nodded and said , "Okay," because I was already strapped into the costume, and the lady was ready to start. What else could I do?

I hid behind the curtain and Miss Thumbelina started telling her story. The way the story went, she said, "Someone will save me!" about twenty times. Then this dopey knight would gallop across the stage yelling, "I'll save you, Princess!"—that was the big joke. That was me. I was the big dopey joke.

Finally, the story was over. Miss Thumbelina made me and my horse come to the center of the stage. I had to hold her hand and take a bow. Then I galloped over behind the curtain and I got out of that costume in about three seconds.

I think I set a new record for blushing that day. Even though there was a show up on the stage, every time I looked around, it felt like half the kids in the auditorium were looking at me. So I tried not to notice. And it worked, because after a while I forgot about my terrible

time on the stage, and I just watched the rest of the stories like everyone else.

At the end of the last story, everybody clapped like crazy. It really was a great assembly. All the teachers stood up, and Mrs. Karp walked onto the stage. She held up her hands and the clapping stopped.

Mrs. Karp said, "I know I speak for everyone when I tell Miss Thumbelina how much we all enjoyed her performance today. Let's all give her one last round of applause."

So we all started clapping and cheering again. Then Mrs. Karp held up her hands again, and the noise stopped, just like turning off a TV.

Mrs. Karp said, "And before I forget, Jake, would you come back up onstage?"

The whole auditorium got quiet except for

some scattered giggling. I turned bright red and walked up onto the stage. Mrs. Karp motioned for me to come and stand beside her. Then she said, "I think we should also give a nice round of applause to our young man of many talents, our own Jake Drake!" And as she said my name, she reached down and patted me on the head.

I'm not sure who started it, but I think it was Ben Grumson. Because when the kids started clapping , someone began saying, "Jake Drake, Jake Drake, Jake Drake," and every kid in the room picked up on it. Four hundred kids started chanting my name.

Then the strangest thing I've ever seen happened. Instead of frowning and stopping the chanting like she could have, Mrs. Karp smiled, and started clapping her hands, and

she chanted along with the kids: "Jake Drake, Jake Drake, Jake Drake!"

I couldn't believe it. I felt like I was in a movie where aliens had taken over a school and made everyone act completely nuts.

After all the kids and teachers and Mrs. Karp had chanted my name about fifteen times, it was starting to feel like the roof might blow off the auditorium. Finally, Mrs. Karp held up her hands and right away the noise stopped. Because even in the middle of a riot, no one would ever mess around with Mrs. Karp.

And then the principal dismissed us to go back to our classroom and get ready for lunch, like nothing strange had happened at all.

So I tried to act that way too. I kept my eyes on the floor and went back toward our classroom. And when some kid in the hallway started

chanting, "Jake Drake, Jake Drake, Jake Drake," I didn't look up. I just kept walking.

I was so glad to be back in my own classroom. It was going to be so good to go to lunch and sit down in a quiet corner with Willie.

I opened my desk to get my lunch, and I gasped. A bunch of kids turned to look at me. I must have sounded like I had seen a ghost. Except it was scarier than that for me. Because I had forgotten. There, under my lunch bag, was the most horrible thing I'd ever seen—that bright orange patrol belt!

I was not going to have a quiet lunch with my best friend. For the second time in one hour, I was going to put on a costume and get on a stage. This time I wasn't going to be a knight in shining armor. This time I had to put on a floppy, orange belt and walk into the

cafeteria. Because every kid in grades three, four, and five was waiting for me. Everyone was waiting for Garbage Guy.

CHAPTER FOUR

Dangerous

I thought about just not wearing the orange patrol belt to lunch. I thought about it for three seconds or so. Then I remembered Mrs. Karp. She would be in the cafeteria too. And she had said I would wear the thing for the rest of the week. I guess she thought wearing the belt was supposed to be an honor. Maybe like having a black belt in karate. Except it wasn't.

So I pulled the thing out of my desk. I looped it over one shoulder, hooked it around my waist, grabbed my lunch, and went out into the hall. Right away a group of fourth-grade girls started to point at me and giggle. But I just held my head up high and walked toward the cafeteria. I kept walking, and I said to myself, *I can live through this. I know I can. I can do this.* And I just pretended that nothing was the matter.

When I got to the cafeteria, I looked for Willie, but he wasn't at our regular table. Then I saw him in the milk line. When I went over to say hi, Willie started talking to me like a spy. He kept looking straight ahead and he tried not to move his lips.

He whispered, "I can't eat with you today."

I whispered back, "How come?"

He said, " Mrs. Karp. She'll know it was

me."

"What do you mean?" I asked.

Willie said, "Me. I left that big mess yesterday."

I said, "But I'll tell her we played Rock, Paper, Scissors, and I lost."

Willie shook his head. "Uh-uh. Better not. See you at recess."

And maybe Willie was right, because Mrs. Karp was already prowling around the lunchroom. She was on the lookout for trashers.

So I got some milk and went to find a place to sit. And as I looked around the cafeteria, it felt like there was a big sign at every table, and the sign said, "No Teacher's Pets Allowed."

Even the table where I usually sat with Willie was filled up. There was only one empty table. And there was a reason it was empty: it was the one next to the teacher's table. Because

at our school the teachers get lunch for free. Except it's not really free. To get a free lunch they have to eat in the cafeteria when their class eats. That was Mrs. Karp's idea to help keep the lunchroom quieter.

So I went to the empty table and sat down. Alone. Just me and my orange patrol belt. And I said to myself, *I can live through this. I know I can. I can do this.*

I opened up my lunch bag, and that made me feel better right away. My mom had packed chocolate pudding *plus* Fig Newtons—two desserts! So I wanted to get the rest of my food out of the way fast. I had just taken a huge bite out of a bologna sandwich, when a voice behind me said, "Is this seat taken? The teacher's table is too crowded today."

It was Miss Cott, my art teacher. And before

I could chew or swallow or say a word, she sat down right next to me, ripped the lid off a Tupperware tub, and started eating a salad that smelled like rotten eggs and onions. And she sat there. Next to me. When she wasn't jamming salad into her mouth, she was smiling at me and chatting away—like she was my best friend or something.

I stopped chewing and looked around the room. About half the kid in the cafeteria were staring at me. Staring at us. At me and Miss Cott. And I could see what they were thinking. It was all over their faces, as plain as grape jelly: *Jake Drake is such a teacher's pet that he even eats lunch with one!*

I finished my sandwich and then ate my two desserts so fast I didn't even taste them. Then I looked sideways at Miss Cott and said,

"Gotta go," and before she could say anything, I grabbed my garbage and left. I went straight across the room, dumped my trash, and went out the side door to the playground.

The first thing I did outside was take off the orange belt and stuff it into my pocket. Because Mrs. Karp never said I had to wear it during recess.

Willie waved at me from the other side of the playground, and I ran over to meet him. The sun was shining, the sky was blue, and birds were singing. It was a beautiful May afternoon, it was recess, and I had survived lunch. I started to feel okay again.

Just before I got to Willie, three fifth graders jumped off the jungle gym and caught up to me.

I stopped and said, "Hi."

The biggest kid looked familiar, but I didn't know his name. He gave me this mean smile and said, "Hey, Garbage Guy—better put your little belt back on. I think I see some trash over there by the fence."

Then the one who was wearing a baseball hat said, "Yeah, and maybe you should get your fake horsie and ride it around the playground for us."

They laughed and high-fived each other, and all three of them got closer and started chanting: "Jake Drake! Jake Drake! Jake Drake! Jake Drake!" Then they got right up into my face. "Jake Drake! Jake Drake! Jake Drake! Jake Drake!" And I just couldn't take it. So I grabbed the guy with the baseball hat and pushed him as hard as I could right into the other two kids. They weren't ready for that,

and all three of them lost their balance and fell down in a heap on the grass. And they stopped chanting my name.

They began to scramble around, trying to get up, and I could see it was time to get out of there. I turned to run, but I bumped into someone. It was Mrs. Karp, standing right there, looking very tall and very angry.

"What's going on here? You boys, get up off the ground this instant!"

Those kids *had* been mean to me, but still, I was the one who pushed first. I was the one who had started fighting. So I said, "Mrs. Karp I..."

And she said, "I know, Jake. You didn't have anything to do with this. Of course not." Then she frowned at the other kids. "You boys, follow me to the office. Now."

And as the fifth graders walked away

behind Mrs. Karp, the one at the end of the line, the biggest one, turned to look at me. He narrowed his eyes and pointed at me, and I could see his mouth move. He didn't make a sound, but I saw what he said. He said, "I'm gonna get you!" and I didn't blame him. It wasn't fair. I was the one who started fighting, but Mrs. Karp didn't see it.

Willie came over and said, "That was awesome! I thought we were going to have to fight all three of them at once!"

I just nodded. Everything had happened so fast.

Willie said, "But I don't think I'd want to be you right now. That big kid? You know who he is, right?"

I shook my head, and Willie said, "No? you don't know who that is? That's Danny Grumson,

Ben's big brother. He's only the toughest kid in the whole school, that's all!"

And standing there on the playground with Willie going on and on about Danny Grumson, something suddenly became very clear to me: Being a teacher's pet can be dangerous. Very dangerous.

CHAPTER FIVE

No More Mr. Nice Guy

The second I got on my bus that afternoon, three or four kids in the back started chanting , "Jake Drake! Jake Drake! Jake Drake!" They probably would have done it forever, but the bus driver turned around and made them stop.

I sat on a seat by myself. Alone. Just like at lunch, but without Miss Cott.

When I got off the bus, I walked the rest of

the way to my house. Alone.

And I didn't feel like a snack, so I went up to my room and I shut the door and flopped flat on my back onto my bed. Alone.

I was feeling pretty sorry for myself. And lying there on my bed, I said what I always say when I feel sorry for myself. I said, "It's not fair!"

And it wasn't. I didn't want to be a teacher's pet. It just happened. I helped Mrs. Snavin with the computer—*Bam!*—teacher's pet. I washed out a couple of paintbrushes—*Bam!*—teacher's pet. I got whomped in gym—*Bam!*—teacher's pet. Cleaned up trash, didn't yell on the bus, helped that storyteller—*Bam! Bam! Bam!*—teacher's pet.

The teachers and even the principal—all of them thought I was so special, so wonderful.

I sat up on my bed. Was I so special and wonderful? Of course not! No way. *But*, if that's what all my teachers *thought*, then that's how they were going to treat me. I'd be *special*, and *sweet*, a real *trooper*.

It was so simple. If my teachers thought I was always so wonderful and so nicey-nice, I'd just have to prove they were making a mistake.

Suddenly I felt great. I jumped off my bed and ran downstairs to get a snack. In the pantry I found a bag of chocolate-chip cookies and I piled about ten of them onto a plate. Then I poured myself a big glass of milk but the carton was really full and I spilled milk all over the counter. I started to grab a paper towel to wipe it up—but then I stopped myself.

I smiled and I dunked a cookie into my glass and I crunched it, and I let the crumbs

fall all over the place. And when I was done eating cookies and spraying crumbs around, I just left everything a mess. I didn't even put the milk back into the refrigerator. And I said to myself, *Now, if this was tomorrow and I was at school, I'd just walk away and leave all this*!

I grinned as I cleaned up the counter and put the milk away. Thinking like that was good practice.

Because tomorrow I wasn't going to be good and clean up after myself. I was going to be bad and rude and unpleasant and messy.

Because on Wednesday, everybody at school was going to see a different Jake Drake.

CHAPTER SIX

Bad Jake

On Wednesday morning as I got on the bus, the driver watched me climb up the steps.

When I was right next to her, she gave me a big smile and said, "How's my favorite little bus rider today?"

I frowned at her and I said, "Terrible. And this bus smells bad!"

The lady got this shocked look on her face.

Then she pushed her lips together, turned her face away, and looked up into her big mirror. She shouted, "Hurry up and sit down back there!" then she slammed the doors shut and grabbed the steering wheel.

As I sat down, I didn't know if I should feel bad or smile. But the important thing was this: That was one bus driver who wasn't going to think Jake Drake was so nicey-nice anymore. And I thought, *Maybe she'll even send me to the principal's office for being rude!* And I was happy about that.

Because that Wednesday, I had to be someone else, someone different. I was going to make some trouble.

When I got off the bus, Willie was waiting for me. We started walking toward the playground because it wasn't time to go inside yet.

This first-grade boy ran right in front of us, and I stuck out my foot. The kid stumbled and rolled onto the grass.

"Hey!" he yelled. And he got up and said, "that wasn't nice!"

I made this mean face at him, and I said, "Yeah? So what?"

The kid was pretty little, so he just frowned and started running again.

Willie looked at me funny. "You okay?"

I said, "No, I'm not okay. All the teachers think I'm so nice, and all the kids think I'm a big teacher's pet." Then I stopped walking and I looked at Willie. I said, "That's what they think, don't they?"

Willie scrunched up his face. "Well...I didn't want to say anything, but, yeah. I heard some kids in my class talking about you yesterday.

They said you want all the teachers to think you're perfect. They said...they said you make them sick. I...I was going to tell them it wasn't true, but then Mrs. Frule looked at us so we had to shut up."

I said, "Well, don't worry about it. Because I'm going to do something about all that. Today."

Willie looked puzzled. "What do you mean?"

"I mean, I'm going to show everybody that I'm not a teacher's pet, that's what."

"But how?" asked Willie.

"I'm just not going to be so nice."

"You mean, like...like tripping that kid?" asked Willie. And when I nodded, he said, "But...if you do stuff like that, you're gonna get in trouble."

I looked at Willie. And I smiled and nodded my head again.

And Willie smiled too. "Ohhh...I get it."

Then the bell rang and kids started for the doors.

Willie said, "Well, have a good day. I mean, have a *bad* day!"

And I grinned and said, "*Real* bad!"

When I got to Mrs. Snavin's room, I threw my jacket into the bottom of my cubby, and then tossed my backpack onto the floor by my desk.

I sat down in my chair and pulled a comic book out of my backpack. I had never read a comic book at school before. It was kind of fun.

When she saw me, Mrs. Snavin came to the back of the room and sat down at the computer closest to my desk. She turned it on the fiddled with it for a minute or two. Then she said, "Jake, this math program is acting up again."

I kept reading my comic book. I pretended not to hear her.

She kept tapping on keys, and than she put her hands in her lap and let out a big sigh. "Jake?" I could tell Mrs. Snavin was looking right at me. "Jake, what should I do?"

Without looking away from my comic book I said, "Take a computer class." That's what I said. Rude. Unhelpful. And I said it loud enough so every kid in the class could hear me.

The room got very quiet. My hands were sweating, and my fingers made spots on the paper of the comic book. Mrs. Snavin was getting furious, I was sure of it. She was getting ready to yell at me, tell me to put away the junk I was reading.

Five seconds passed.

Then Mrs. Snavin stood up slowly and walked over to my desk. I felt her standing there,

a little too close. I gulped, ready for the worst. She reached out her hand to grab my comic book.

Except she didn't.

Instead, she patted me on the head. "Jake, you are *absolutely* right! I've just been putting it off and putting it off, and now, thanks to you, that's *just* what I'm going to do. I'm going to sign up for a computer class today—this *very* afternoon! Because if I can't run the computers in my own classroom, then I guess I have no business using them. So we'll just forget about the computers for a while. After all, who says we need computers to learn about number lines anyway? I have stacks and stacks of perfectly good worksheets. Jake, you're *wonderful!* I don't know what I'd do without you!"

Ben Grumson gave me this dirty look. And

so did about twenty other kids. Because now instead of using the computers for math, we were going to have to do worksheets. I mean, the math game was pretty stupid, but we still got to use a computer. Which is a lot better than worksheets.

Then Mrs. Snavin said, "Jake, could you go to the office for me and ask Mrs. Drinkwater for the community college catalog?"

I just kept reading my comic book, and I said, "I'm reading." Not nice at all. My hands were still sweating.

And what does Mrs. Snavin say? Does she say, "Listen here, young man! You put down that trash and do what I tell you to!"? Does she grab me by the arm and say, "I don't like the tone of your voice, Mr. Drake! We better talk to the principal about this!"?

No. right away Mrs. Snavin says, "Why of course. How *rude* of me. Here you are doing some extra reading before class even starts, and I'm interrupting you. You've always been such a *good* reader! I'll send someone else." And she did.

That's when I decided I would have to try harder. I wasn't being bad enough.

After attendance and the Pledge of Allegiance, Mrs. Snavin said, "All right, class. For reading today, let's begin by talking about the story we finished yesterday. Let's see...Karl, what's one thing you liked about 'Tom's Pet Crow'?"

Karl sat up straighter in his chair and said, "Well, I kind of liked the way Tom taught the crow how to..."

Right while Karl was talking, I just butted in, and I said, "I didn't like anything about that

story."

Mrs. Snavin's eyebrows went up. "Nothing? My goodness, Jake. You shouldn't have interrupted Karl...but maybe you should tell us one thing you *didn't* like."

I said, "The whole story was stupid. And boring. And I didn't like it. At all."

"Well!" said Mrs. Snvin. "Hoe about the rest of you? Is there anyone else who didn't like the story?"

I looked around, and almost every kid's hand went up in the air. And I thought, *Hey! Look! I'm a leader! They agree with me. And they can see that I'm not the teacher's pet! Hurrah!*

Mrs. Snavin looked around, and then she looked at me, and she took a deep breath and let it out slowly. And I thought, *Uh-oh. Now I'm going to get it!*

Then she smiled. At me. And she said, "Jake, you are *so* right! I didn't like this story very much, either. That'll teach me to pay more attention to what's good and what's not! So let's skip ahead in our reading books...all the way to page 287."

While we were flipping pages, Mrs. Snavin said, "Now, this is a longer story, so you won't have time to finish it during reading time. But you can take it home and finish it tonight. And I hope you'll like this story better, because, like Jake says, a story should never be boring or stupid. Right now, I want everyone to take out a piece of paper and write down three ways you think 'Tom's pet Crow' could be better."

All around the class, kids were groaning and giving me dirty looks. Because now we had to do some writing. *And* we had homework, *and*

it was all my fault. Plus, Mrs. Snavin was still smiling at me and saying how smart I was.

And I was starting to wonder, *How bad do I have to be to make her stop treating me like her little sweetie pie?* Because being bad isn't as easy as some kids make it look.

A little later during art class, Miss Cott came over and looked at the painting I was making for Mother's Day. She stood there a minute, and then she said, "Jake, that is so *sweet!* I think that's just about the *sweetest* Mother's Day painting I've ever seen!"

Before art, I didn't know how I was going to be bad in Miss Cott's class. But when she said that, I knew just what to do. I grabbed the bottom of my painting and I pulled the paper out of the clips on the easel. I ripped it up and I said, "Well, I think it's a rotten painting!" Real

loud. And then I grabbed the little brush I had been using and I snapped it right in half.

Miss Cott stood there with her mouth open. Every kid in the class was looking at her, waiting for an explosion. Then she took a deep breath and sat down in a chair. She started nodding her head. Then in a soft voice she said, "Class, I want you all to pay attention." Which is something she didn't need to say. She was still nodding her head. I thought she was going to start screaming any second. She looked around at the class and said, "Jake has just been *very* brave. You see, I said I liked his painting, and what did Jake do? He tore it up! He *knows* he can do better work than that, and he's not afraid to tear up his work and start over! Jake, I think you might be the *best* art student in this whole school!" And then Miss Cott smiled at

me like I had just painted the Mona Lisa or something. So art class was a bust. I was still the teacher's pet.

One of Mr. Collins's big rules is "Never Swing on the Ropes." So what did I do at the beginning of gym class? I swung on the ropes, and I yelled, "Yahoooo!" while I was doing it. And when Mr. Collins came through the doorway and saw me, what did he do? Did he come and grab me? Did he shake his fist at me? No. he grinned. Then he said, "I was wondering who'd be the first kid to break that rule this year. I love a kid who's got some *spirit,* some *backbone!* The rest of you kids could take a lesson from Drake here. Okay, trooper, off that rope, and give me five push-ups. And the next kid who swings will do thirty push-ups *and* thirty sit-ups, so the rest of you, don't get any

ideas."

Then at lunch when I headed the orange belt to Mrs. Karp and said, "I don't want to wear this anymore," did I get in trouble? No. Mrs. Karp patted me on the head and announced something to everyone in the cafeteria. She smiled at me and said Jake Drake was being very unselfish. She said Jake Drake wanted share the *fun* of wearing the lunch patrol belt with someone else. And then she gave the belt to Ben Grumson. Who did not smile at me.

And no one was happy with me during afternoon math time, either, because we all had to do three worksheets. Instead of using the computers. Because of me.

So by the end of school on Wednesday afternoon, I was ready to give up. All day I had been about as bad and rude as I knew how to

be. And it hadn't done any good. I was still the teacher's pet. *Every* teacher's pet.

After school as I got on the bus, this wave of lemon smell rolled down the stairs at me. Then I saw three yellow air fresheners hanging from the back of the driver's seat. Before I could get past her, the bus driver grabbed me and gave me a big hug.

She said, "After what you said this morning, well, I went right out and bought these things for the bus. And when I went to take care of my little grandson today, he climbed up on my lap and he said, 'Gamma mells good!' Isn't that the cutest thing you ever heard?!" Then the lady hugged me again. With everyone watching. And she said, "You're still my favorite little passenger!"

No doubt about it: I had a one-way ticket to Petsville.

CHAPTER SEVEN

Bad Dream, Good Idea

Wednesday night I had a dream.

I was in a cage, a little wire cage in a room. I was on my hands and knees. There were two bowls inside my cage. One of them was filled with Cheerios and the other one had root beer. Every once in awhile I would bend down and eat a mouthful of cereal, and then lick up some root beer. All around me there were little cages

with other kids in them. Mark was in one, and Ben Grumson, and there was Marsha, and Karl—even Willie. All of us were munching cereal and lapping up soda.

Then this tall lady came into the room. She bent down and looked in every cage. She looked in Marsha's cage, and when she did, she frowned and said, "No!" Then she looked in at Ben, and she frowned and said, "No!" She looked into every cage and she kept saying, "No! No! No!"

Then she bent down and looked into my cage, and she smiled and said, "Yes!" and she opened my cage and put an orange dog collar around my neck. And she held out a Fig Newton and said, "Good Boy!" And when I sat up, she put the Fig Newton in my mouth. I started to chew the Fig Newton. Then the tall lady bent down and patted me on the head. And she said,

"Now you're my little pet!" And when I looked into the lady's face, it was Mrs. Karp!

I sat up in my bed and I grabbed at my neck and I started yelling, "No! No! Take this collar off me! I'm not your pet! No! Nooo!"

And that's when my dad came into my room and turned on the light.

"Easy, Jake, it's all right." Dad sat on my bed, and he held on to my arm. "It's all right, Jake. You were just having a dream, that's all. You're Jake, and I'm your dad, and we're right here in our own house, and you're awake now, and everything's all right." I was shaking and I was all sweaty. And Dad kept holding on to my arm. I was so glad he was there.

When I was totally awake, Dad said, "Bad dream, huh?"

I nodded. "Yeah. A nightmare." And I

shivered. Then I said, "Dad, were you ever a teacher's pet?"

He said, "Hmm. Let me think⋯yes, I think I was, once. Back when I was in sixth grade."

My eyes opened wide. "Really? Did you *want* to be?"

Dad smiled. "Did I want to be? Yes, I suppose I did. My English teacher was a lady named Mrs. Palmer, and she was very smart. And I guess I thought she was pretty, too. My friend Tim and I stayed after class sometimes to help erase the chalkboards and straight up her room, little things like that. So, I guess we were *both* teacher's pets."

I frowned. "And did she treat you and your friend special? Or let you get away with stuff?"

Dad thought a second, and then nodded. "Yes, I think she did, at least a little bit. I

remember one time when I didn't do my homework and Mrs. Palmer caught me. She frowned at me and scolded me in class and said I had to come in after school. But when I went after school, she just smiled and said, 'Now, you won't do that again, will you, Jimmy?' and I said, 'No.' and then she let me leave. And I always did my homework after that too."

"But what about the other kids?" I asked. "Didn't they hate you for being the teacher's pet?"

Dad scratched his head, which made his hair look even more messed up. He said, "I don't really remember. All I remember is how Mrs. Palmer used to smile at me sometimes."

I said, "But what if you had a lot of teachers, and they were all being super nice to you, and you didn't even like the way they smiled, and

then all the kids thought you were trying to be all goody-goody. What about that?"

"Well..." And then Dad gave this really big yawn. "If I was *trying* to get the teachers to treat me special, then I guess the kids would be right. Because that would be like I was trying to get away with something. But if a teacher decides to be nicer to you than she is to some other kid, then that's not your fault. That's the teacher's fault. Because a teacher's not supposed to be nicer to one kid than she is to another, right?"

I nodded and Dad said, "Now listen. You lean back on your pillow, and shut your eyes and go back to sleep, all right?" And he pulled my covers up under my chin, and kissed me on the cheek, and then got up and shut off the light. "Good night, Jake."

"G'night, Dad."

"Sleep tight."

Then I was alone again. And I kept thinking. Because Dad was right. A teacher's not supposed to be nicer to one kid than she is to another. Or a principal, either. And I wasn't trying to be a teacher's pet. I was just being myself. So it wasn't my fault. And even when I had tried to be bad, that hadn't worked, either, because— because I'm *not* bad, and everyone knows it.

And then I got a big idea. It was big, and it was simple. But would it work? Maybe it was too simple.

There was only one way to find out. And only one place, too, and that was school. On Thursday. So first I had to go back to sleep. And that's what I did.

And I didn't have any more dreams about orange dog collars.

CHAPTER EIGHT

Not So Special

Trying out a new plan can be scary. But if you don't try it out, you can't find out if it's going to work.

So Thursday morning right after attendance and the Pledge of Allegiance and the announcements, I put my hand up and waited for Mrs. Snavin to call on me.

She said, "Yes, Jake?"

And I took a deep breath and I said, "Mrs. Snavin? You know how you were having trouble with the computers? Well, I think that if we wanted to use them for math today, then you should really ask Shelley. She knows a lot more about computers than I do. And Ben, too. He's good with programs. They could really help. Then maybe we could use the computers for math, even before you finish your computer class. Because they're a lot more fun to use than worksheets."

Mrs. Snavin said, "Maybe after reading there'll be some time to work on them. Does that sound good to everyone?"

And a lot of the kids in the class nodded and said, "Yes."

Then Mrs. Snavin said, "That was a good idea, Jake. Thank you." And she smiled at me.

And I didn't care if she smiled at me, because it *was* a good idea. And I didn't care if the whole class saw her smile at me, because there's nothing wrong with being glad about a good idea, right? And sharing a good idea didn't make me a teacher's pet, right? It just made me myself.

And that was my big idea. From the night before. To just be myself and not think about being a teacher's pet. Because if I know I'm *not* a teacher's pet, then I'm not. Right?

But it's tricky, because if you get treated special, everyone will still think you're a teacher's pet. That's what kids hate, when a kid gets treated special. Because it's not fair. And it's really not. Because a teacher is supposed to treat all the kids the same.

After reading, Mrs. Snavin had to send

some lunch money to the office, and I asked her if I could take it. Not because I was a teacher's pet. I wanted to go to the office for another reason.

When I got to the office, I gave the money to the school secretary, and then I said, "Is Mrs. Karp busy?"

Mrs. Drinkwater looked at me from behind the counter and said, "Yes, Jake. Just sit down over there for a minute."

So I sat down and gulped, because even when you're not in trouble, waiting to see the principal is no fun.

A couple of minutes later, Mrs. Karp came out, and when she saw me, she got this big smile on her face. She said, "Come into my office, Jake." And when I did, she sat down. And I was glad she did. Mrs. Karp is so tall that

she's extra scary until she sits down. Then she asked, "Now, what can I do for you?"

I gulped again, and I said, "I'm having a problem. Ever since Monday, things have been happening to me. Things that make all the other kids think I'm a big teacher's pet."

Then I stopped to look at her face. I wanted to make sure she didn't look mad or anything. And she didn't, so I kept talking. "Because, I'm *not* a teacher's pet. I'm just a regular kid. But if everyone thinks I am, then that's bad, right?"

Mrs. Karp nodded her head slowly, and said, "Yes...I can see how that would be a problem. And teachers should not be giving special privileges to children. Are some teachers treating you special?"

And I said, "Well, kind of. Sometimes. I think."

And Mrs. Karp leaned forward in her chair and said, "Really? When? And who?"

And I gulped extra hard and I said, "Like on Tuesday. With...with you."

"What? What are you talking about?" Mrs. Karp looked kind of angry, but I couldn't stop in the middle.

So I told her. About me starting that fight on the playground, about pushing that fifth grader. And about how the other kids got in trouble and I didn't. Because she said she knew that it wasn't my fault. When it really was.

Mrs. Karp leaned back again and put her fingertips together. "Ah. Yes. I can see how that would be a problem—even though I didn't see you push anyone. And before that, the assembly...and then the lunchroom business. My goodness! This has been quite a week for

you, hasn't it, Jake?"

And I nodded and said, "Yeah. Really."

Mrs. Karp stood up and walked around her desk. "Well, you'd better get back to class, Jake. I'll do some thinking about this. Maybe we can talk some more at lunchtime."

"At lunchtime?" I asked. "Should I come to the office then?"

Mrs. Karp was quiet a moment, and then she said, "No. I'll come and find you, all right? And I'm glad you were brave enough to come and talk to me."

And I could tell Mrs. Karp kind of wanted to pat me on the head. But she didn't. and I was glad.

When I got back to the classroom, it was free period. Some kids were reading, some were drawing or building with LEGO blocks, and

Shelley and Ben were working on the computers.

I went back and stood next to Ben, looking over his shoulder at the screen. When he saw me, I asked, "Fixed it yet?"

He didn't take his eyes off the screen. "Yeah. It was simple. But I'm pretending it's real hard. That way, I might get to come in over lunchtime. Then I can play a game." Ben took his hand off the keys and reached into his pocket. Looking around to be sure Mrs. Snavin wasn't watching, he pulled out a CD-ROM and showed it to me. It was BATTLE TANX. "I always have a copy of this with me, just in case." And he grinned.

It was Thursday, so we didn't have art or gym. After free time, we watched a social studies video about these explorers name Lewis and Clark, and it was like this long

adventure story, except it was all true. The morning was going great. And the best part was I could tell the kids in my class didn't think I was the teacher's pet anymore.

But the minute I went out into the hallway to go to lunch, some kids from Mrs. Frule's class saw me and this boys said, "Hey, look! It's Jakey Drakey. Gonna eat lunch with your girlfriend Miss Cott today?"

And then three or four fifth-grade kids started saying, "Jake Drake! Jake Drake! Jake Drake!" And one of the boys knocked my lunch out of my hands, and an apple rolled out of the bag.

I wanted to start punching people, but I didn't. As I picked up my lunch and headed for the cafeteria, I thought, *Maybe things are better in my own classroom, but what about all the other*

kids? And all the other teachers?

It felt like everyone else in the school was going to think I was a teacher's pet for the rest of my life.

CHAPTER NINE

Crash Landing, but Safe

The lunchroom wasn't any better. In the milk line, a fourth grader asked me how come I wasn't cleaning tables yet. Then a fifth-grade kid said, "Hey, look! It's the original Garbage Guy!"

And when I was walking over to where Willie was sitting, a girl in Mrs. Frule's class said, "Hey, Jake—Miss Cott was talking about

you in art class today. She says you are so *sweet*!" And then a whole bunch of girls started to giggle.

I sat down and tossed Willie his chocolate milk. I said, "Hi. So you think it's safe to sit with me today?"

"Yeah. I think so. Looks like you're still famous."

I nodded and bit into my peanut butter sandwich. "Yeah. Guess I'm gonna have to learn to live with it."

I learned my head back to take a long drink of milk, but I stopped. Something was wrong with Willie, with his face. Willie looked like one of those kids in *Jurassic Park* when the Tyrannosaurus rex is trying to eat their car. I put my milk carton down and said, "What's wrong?"

And Willie whispered, "Mrs. Karp. Coming

this way. Fast."

I turned around, and Willie wasn't kidding. Mrs. Karp was headed across the cafeteria. Every kid was watching her. She had this awful look on her face, and she was walking fast. And in a straight line. Toward us.

She came right up to me, and I could feel my face turn white. My heart was pounding. Mrs. Karp glared down at me. She was so tall, and it was like her face was made of stone.

Without saying a word, she reached down and took hold of my arm right above the elbow. Then real loud, she said, "You are coming to the office with me. Right now!"

Willie looked like he wanted to crawl under the table.

Then Mrs. Karp turned around and started walking. She was still holding on to my arm,

and it probably looked like she was dragging me across the cafeteria. And as we walked past with everyone staring at me, in this loud voice Mrs. Karp said, "We have some things to talk about, young man. About the *ropes* in gym class. And about your *behavior* in the art room. And about something that happened Tuesday out on the *playground.*" I looked up, and at one of the lunch tables, Danny Grumson was smiling at me and nodding his head. Then he put out his pointer finger and pulled it—*zip*—straight across his throat.

As Mrs. Karp pulled me across the big room, I felt myself start to blush. And I thought, *That's the last time I'll ever trust a principal. I thought I was so smart to go and talk to her. Now she's probably going to call my mom and dad, too.*

Then we were out the door, down the steps,

along the front hallway, and into her office.

I hate it when I feel like I'm going to cry. Especially at school. But that's how I felt. I kept my eyes on the floor. I sat in the chair in front of Mrs. Karp's desk, and when I heard her sit in her chair, I looked up at her.

Then I looked away real quick, and then looked back again. Because I couldn't believe my eyes. Mrs. Karp was smiling. A big, warm, friendly smile.

I kept staring at her and she said, "How was that?"

I shook my head. "What? How was what?"

"My performance. How did you like my performance?" And Mrs. Karp kept on smiling. "I guess it was pretty good if it fooled you, too. Sorry, but I had to make it look real."

I shook my head, still trying to understand.

"Then you're not…mad at me?"

She shook her head, still smiling. "No. Not at all. Remember this morning when I told you I'd think about your…problem? Well, I did. And what just happened, that was my solution."

And that's when I got it. It was all an act. I said, "But the ropes in gym class? I really did that."

Mrs. Karp said, "I talked with Mr. Collins, and he understands everything—and you *will* be doing more push-ups and sit-ups. Tomorrow."

"And art class?" I asked.

"Yes, Miss Cott will be making quite a big speech to you on Friday about how wrong it was to destroy school property. Which is true, of course. You shouldn't have broken that paintbrush."

Then Mrs. Karp looked at her watch. "Well, I think it's safe for you to go back and have the

rest of your lunch now. But remember, Jake, this has to be our secret, or it's going to look like I've given you *special treatment*—and we wouldn't want anyone to think *that*, now, would we?"

And at the moment, if Mrs. Karp had wanted to pat me on the head, I wouldn't have minded it one bit.

So that was how the longest four days of my life finally ended. And I never told anyone about Mrs. Karp's great performance, not even Willie.

The rest of my lunch tasted great that Thursday. And I wish you could have seen the way everyone looked at me when I walked back into the cafeteria and sat down to eat.

Some kids looked at me like I was an escaped criminal. Some kids looked at me like I was a

hero coming back from a war. Some kids looked at me like they were afraid to look at me. But nobody—not one kid, not one teacher, not one cafeteria lady—looked at me like I had ever been Jake Drake, teacher's Pet.